TO :

NEXT!

I hope your scared isn't as crazy as mine!

NEXT!

The Search for My Last
First Date

Robert James

Library of Congress Control Number: 2014909247
ISBN: Hardcover   978-1-4990-2204-9
                 Softcover   978-1-4990-2205-6
                 eBook   978-1-4990-2203-2

This is a work of fiction. Names, characters, places and incidents either are the product of the author's imagination or are used fictitiously, and any resemblance to any actual persons, living or dead, events, or locales is entirely coincidental.

Any people depicted in stock imagery provided by Thinkstock are models, and such images are being used for illustrative purposes only.
Certain stock imagery © Thinkstock.

Print information available on the last page.

Rev. date: 10/07/2015

To order additional copies of this book, contact:
Xlibris
1-888-795-4274
www.Xlibris.com
Orders@Xlibris.com
619421

CONTENTS

"Any man who can drive safely while kissing a pretty girl is simply not giving the kiss the attention it deserves."

—Albert Einstein

FOREWORD

"Bob, Please give me a call just as soon as possible!"

I was starting to panic. A potentially bad situation had developed, and now we appeared to be on a collision course with disaster.

Bob, of course, called me back almost immediately even though I hadn't talked with him in a couple of years. He was laughing when I answered the phone, and he greeted me with "What in the world is wrong *now?*" The more I told him, the harder he laughed.

You have to know more about Bob before you read this book, so please indulge me a moment.

He and I have been friends for most of our adult lives. We met in college. I was madly in love with Bob's roommate, best friend, and fraternity brother, Bill. Consequently, the three of us spent lots of time together.

We all finally graduated, and Bill and I got married—just not to each other. Neither of our marriages lasted. Fortunately, several years ago, Bill and I found an opportunity to reconnect; and it was a joy to discover we could renew and continue to enjoy our friendship.

I was excited recently when Bill and his new wife made the trip for a short stay at a nearby beach. Bob hadn't seen Bill in fifteen years. The four of us planned on meeting for lunch the day after they arrived in town.

My panicked call to Bob was made from my car on my way to the restaurant an hour away . . .

"It's *bad*, Bob! Bill's wife hates me, and she's mean about it! And she doesn't even try to hide it!" I didn't get it. I tried to make a fuss over her, letting her know how much we appreciated her making Bill, well, ridiculously happy.

Bob assured me there was no reason to worry. He would take control of the situation—even serving as a human shield should the need arise.

The lunch had only been scheduled a couple of days before, and Bob had juggled several appointments to make sure he was there. Given my call and concern, he cleared yet another meeting to guarantee he arrived at the restaurant first and effectively set the tone as the host.

Bob was right—it all worked out. He was the consummate gentleman. He was relaxed and made it comfortable and fun, immediately diffusing any tension. The three of us laughed and told stories and laughed harder. Mrs. Bill even succumbed to Bob's charm and participated in the conversation.

When I called Bob, practically in tears and without a clue about how to proceed, he took the bull by the horns. Bob instinctively operates as a Dragon Slayer.

There is another reason why that day is memorable. Bob announced he had written a book—a real book— with interest from a publisher and a screenplay writer.

Huh?

Yes, he had written a book. It was based upon the crazy "true life adventures" he experienced as he forged his way into the current dating culture. Bob shared with us a few of the stories. They were really funny and kind of shocking. Things had changed a lot since we were in college. He also offered to allow each of us to read an advance copy of the book. Doing so was a privilege, and I couldn't wait to start.

But more about Bob. Our college required all students to dine exclusively in the school cafeteria. Breakfast. Lunch. Dinner. Seven days a week. Initially drawn together at a seating arrangement at the fraternity table, Bill, Bob, and I usually ended up sitting directly across the table from one another more often than not. In much the same way as siblings sharing the family table, we developed a rather complex bond. We learned about ourselves, and we learned about each other. We also made the most of the opportunity it provided as a platform upon which to hone our "verbal sparring" skills, and Bob was good—sometimes he left me speechless.

There were times when we argued like cats and dogs. There were times when we did not like one another and times when we loved each other. We poked fun at one another, and we bragged about ourselves, just like family. Throughout all of these experiences, whether they were conversations, confrontations, or just out having a good time, one thing remained constant: Bob was *always* a gentleman.

In every sense of the word, Bob was, and remains to this day, a true gentleman. It is simply who he is. There are so few like him; it's easy for him to stand out. Manners, class, confidence, wit, charm—a true gentleman.

At the age of twenty, Bob was intentionally communicating his respect for and appreciation of the women playing a role in his life. And not just with the girls he dated or wanted to date.

It's one of those odd things that sticks out in your memory—that college cafeteria, thirty years ago, more or less—the kitchen staff preparing, serving, and cleaning up after all of those wonderful meals. That group of ladies absolutely *adored* "Bobby."

An oversized employee bulletin board hung on the wall near the back of the dining area. Decorated to match the seasons, it was covered with updates, opportunities, announcements, etc. Smack dab in the center of that board one day was a great big picture of the man they referred to as "Our Bobby."

I am dead serious. Those ladies encountered hundreds and hundreds of students numerous times a day, every day, year after year. Bob stood out from the crowd. They loved him. They even baked cookies for him. Bob was just friendly and quite charming.

I had a chance to talk with several of the ladies who were a part of this fan club once after we had all graduated. They said it was rather simple. They knew

Bob genuinely appreciated them. He understood they made a conscious effort to prepare those elaborate meals several times a day. He thanked them every single day—for years. Bob said it doesn't take a lot of effort to be nice to anyone.

Which brings me back to the book.

I began reading the book the day after we had lunch. I simply could not put it down until I finished it that evening. Even though I was by myself, I was a tad embarrassed to catch myself laughing out loud time and time again.

But reading it was also terrifying. In his book, I think he exposed almost every insecurity and self-consciousness I have about men, dating, relationships, and probably a few I didn't know I had. It's scarier out there than most of us would likely imagine. How he thinks about dating was eye-opening. And I hated to learn that it apparently isn't uncommon for some women to lack self-respect on even a basic level. Not having been in a relationship for a while and not searching, Bob's book convinced me that while the dating world could be a very difficult place to navigate, the end prize of love and happiness makes it worth the effort.

I'm sure he would deny it, but most of the women who read this book will agree . . . Bob is Prince Charming personified.

Bob considers the book to be a comedy. While it is very funny, I urge you to take my word for it: the book is actually a modern-day romantic *fairytale*. Bob is the unsure hero on a quest to find a princess to love and to cherish.

Bob finds himself alone. He dreams of finding a partner men assume would be the ideal. As he kisses them along the way, it becomes apparent they are frogs in disguise. He ends up finding happiness with a regular, good, loving woman. She lives a balanced life. She is one of us.

You are going to enjoy this book. I promise.

Catherine C.

INTRODUCTION

I walked out of the courthouse after appearing before the judge to finalize my divorce, and I wrote a check to my attorney, which about wiped out my account. She got everything, including the friends. I drove home thinking about where I was in life and hoping I had enough gas to get home. I'm a social guy, and I had really been lonely even before I was on my own. I started to think about what life had in store for me next.

I had been faithful in a long-term marriage and had a nice home. I left with nothing except my clothes. I now lived in a house with no furniture. I had a TV on the floor and watched it from a folding camp chair. I slept on an air mattress, ate off paper plates and used plastic utensils, and only had a frying pan and a cookie sheet to cook with. I was starting over. I saved money, and the first furniture I bought was a bed for my daughters when they spent the night. My youngest daughter told me I could sleep in her bed when she wasn't there instead of on the air mattress.

I'm a businessman, well-educated, and have three kids in high school and college. I go to church semi-regularly (but I'm no saint), and have moderately conservative morals and am told I'm a great guy. I thought I was decent-looking. I had coached my kids' sports teams, been a scout leader, and took my kids to church. I went to all their games, school events, and recitals.

I was raised in a southern, military family with "Yes, sirs" and "No, ma'ams" and proper manners. I was taught to treat a woman with respect. And unlike Tucker Max, I have a conscience.

In my forties, with a few extra pounds, I had concerns—I hadn't dated in well over twenty years. Could I get the mojo back? Were all the good girls already taken? Holy crap! What was I going to do? I had to get back into shape!

If I did find women who had potential, would they find me interesting? Attractive? Sexy? I'm a pretty confident guy, have a good job, know lots of people. But what did I know about women and dating? I thought about dating the same way I did in college. But I was going to soon find out things had changed—a lot. Where was I supposed to start?

I saw what my kids were doing—hanging out, casual get-togethers, going out in groups. But they never seemed to have one-on-one dates that I saw. Had dating changed that much? I didn't have many close friends, and the ones I did have were married and didn't want a single guy hanging around. Hook-ups, friends with benefits, third date rule—so much to learn about. I wasn't looking for a one-night stand; I really wanted a girlfriend.

So where was I going to meet nice, attractive, classy women? I had few ideas on how I could get started. Against what the little voice inside me said, I went by myself into what I thought was a nicer bar one night—the Blue Martini. I got there and felt like I was in a meat market. I was offered drinks, asked to dance, hit on, and propositioned, all within the time to finish a glass of wine. There were all types of women there—small ones, big ones, most in their mid-thirties to mid-fifties, some smelled like an ash tray, some were drunk, some sloppy drunk, some had funny lines, most had a friend or two with them. The one common characteristic seemed to be a sense of desperation. By the time I left, I felt slimed. It quickly confirmed my belief that you can't meet a nice girl hanging out in a bar—even a nice bar. This was not for me. There had to be a better way.

At work the day after the Blue Martini, I told a guy in my office about my adventure. Chris was thirty-five, divorced about five years, and was very active socially— no, he was a player. He took me to lunch, and we talked about how he was going to help me find a girl. I told him I didn't want to find a girl; I wanted to find the right girl. Chris said I had to meet a lot of women to find the right one, and the best way to filter though a lot of women was online.

He told me how to find and meet women online and said he had the most success on Match.com. He had been on other dating sites, but this one was the best. If a woman wasn't willing to pay $30/month to be on Match versus a free site, Chris reasoned, she probably isn't the kind of woman we would probably want to meet.

I was very skeptical. He said he'd show me, so we went back to the office. Chris signed on to his Match. com account, and he showed me how many women in our area were on the site. There were hundreds and hundreds, all with pictures, information about their interests, something about themselves, and what they were looking for in a man. I was amazed. It was like I was coming out of the dark ages.

Chris showed me how many women had sent him messages through Match's messaging and how they initially communicated. After a message or two, they would exchange phone numbers; and after a conversation or two, they may arrange a meeting if there was an interest. There were ways to filter through them and to find women who had similar interests, similar beliefs, even those who were looking for a guy like me—all within my city! It was like shopping in an online catalog for a woman! Okay, I can do this. So Chris and I set up my profile and added a few pictures.

Chris warned me that through his experience, not everyone on the site is completely honest in who they say they are and what they really look like—and they may embellish the facts a little. My thinking was why would someone wanting to meet someone for a possible relationship want to start it off by lying? I guess I was naïve or that much out of touch.

My inbox started to get messages. I responded. I read through women's profiles—lots of them—and I was overwhelmed. They listed what they were looking for in a man. Several wanted someone to give them the good life. Others said they were looking for someone who *must* love their dogs, cats, children, Jesus, Thai food, their ex mother-in-law, horses, country music, scuba diving, long walks on the beach, snow skiing, tequila, karaoke, bull riding, or Harley Davidsons. One said her date must be able to hold their breath for at least sixty seconds—what is that all about?

Wow! I didn't own a Harley, I've never been scuba diving, I fall down snow-covered mountains, I couldn't sing, and tequila, well, it's not a friend of mine. Bull riding? Really?

One woman's profile said she was looking for Mr. Wonderful and described him like a superhero— tall, dark, handsome, fit, and successful. Her profile also said she was a few pounds overweight, had four children at home and horses, dogs, cats, and snakes. Her pictures weren't particularly flattering. Not trying to be mean, but I wondered why Mr. Wonderful would be interested in her.

I had in my profile that I was interested in meeting women within fifteen miles of my house. I got messages from women across the country—Russia, Ukraine, London, and China. Still, I pushed on, taking a chance putting myself out there in an online profile.

I initiated contact with some women, and some responded! Contact with some women ended with the messages, though. Messages I received like "Hey, you're cute," "What are you doing Friday night?" "My husband likes to watch," or "My green card expires in three weeks" tended to turn me off. So did the "I've never been married, but I have four kids" or "How much do you make?" I got several "I'll show you mine if you show me yours" type of messages. I also quickly learned that if I gave my personal e-mail out, there was a possibility I was going to soon get a picture of a woman in some state of undress—usually taken in her bathroom mirror.

After messaging back and forth a few times with a woman online, I would talk on the phone to some who seemed interesting. Later, I would go more for the ones who seemed less interesting and more "normal."

I usually didn't share my last name until when we met. As soon as I learned a woman's name, I would Google her. You can't be too careful. Google searches halted my interest in women a few times. I found a couple of DUI arrests, a drunk and disorderly arrest, and a fairly recent shoplifting charge. Mostly, I found interesting things, like awards, news articles, and things like that which gave me more to talk about when I met them.

This book is a collection of some of my meetings and encounters with some of these women, the majority of which were first dates. Most of the women I met are from the dating site while a few were met in other ways. I really did date these different women over a couple of years. I hope you have fun with the stories from these dates. As they say, the truth is often funnier than fiction.

If you happen to be one of the women I dated in one of these stories, your name was changed to protect your identity and, in some cases, to protect you from getting Baker Acted. So please don't sue me.

And thanks for buying the book. I need the money to help pay my credit card bill for all those dates— dating is expensive!

ONLINE PROFILE

"About Me and What I'm Looking For" was the heading on one's Match.com profile where you could write whatever you wanted people to know about you. It's hard to describe yourself, but I tried my best. I sat for hours thinking about what to say. Here's what I came up with:

Chemistry and timing—they're tough to get right at the same time.

I am described as a confident guy and a gentleman, definitely easygoing and easy to talk with, and am told I have a good sense of humor. I work hard, but like to have fun too. My pictures are fairly current, and I'm often told I look better in person.

Looking for someone special who enjoys dining, travel, and beaches; someone who likes to go out in little black dresses or a pair of jeans, or just lounge around in a comfortable pair of shorts; someone who is comfortable at a black-tie dinner, a play on Broadway, or a barbecue. I'm looking for an attractive, feminine woman who likes being treated like a woman and is comfortable in many social settings while having fun. I like women who appreciate a guy's attempt at romance, who can be affectionate and sensual, and may like to be spoiled a little.

I really like a good glass of wine. I enjoy things from the arts to college football. I'm looking for someone special to have fun with, who has a good sense of humor, is easygoing, has diverse interests, and knows that I have a great relationship with my children. Sorry, I don't have a Harley or a tattoo—nor do I want one.

Definitely not into the bar scene, but I like going out especially for live music, from a major concert to a guy with a guitar on a beach deck somewhere or a nice wine bar. I love to cook but hate doing it for one. I eat a bowl of cereal over my sink for dinner too often.

I have a great job that I enjoy. I'm a stable guy. I don't have time for games. I can be a loyal friend—and more. Thanks for taking time to read this. I hope your pictures are less than a few years old. Please be honest with your age and body type. Serial daters, please pass on by. If you don't have a picture, I won't respond. And I only like winks in person.

TAKE ME NOW

I hadn't done much dating and really didn't go out much. My assistant, Jenny, and her husband were throwing a party at her house and invited me. I knew I should get out more. I had worked together with her for ten years and was friends with her husband and family, and I knew some people who would be there, so I decided to go.

Jenny was more than my assistant—she was my friend, probably my best friend. Spending ten hours a day, five days a week for ten years together, you tend to develop a good relationship. Jenny was a great friend; she looked out for me, protected me, and gave me advice whether I wanted it or not. She was always upbeat and supportive, and she knew pretty much everything about me. She was with me through my promotions, my divorce, and the death of my mom. She helped me professionally and personally. I probably wasn't as good of a friend to her, but I tried.

I went to her party and was having a good time. One of her girlfriends was flirting with me, and then she said something to me in front of Jenny that changed me. She said I dressed like a married man! I asked her what she was talking about. She told me my jeans were too baggy (they were comfortable!) and my shirt was boring (yes, comfortable). I was almost offended but kind of understood what she was saying.

"Mandy! Doesn't he need some better pants?" Jenny asked. Jenny's sister, Liz, agreed.

"And a shirt," Mandy said.

Mandy had been out of college about five years, and we had become friends. She was so cute. She was always upbeat with a great smile. I loved being around her; she was a lot of fun. We occasionally flirted playfully, and it was all innocent.

By now, several women were looking at my pants, supporting Jenny, her friend, Liz and Mandy.

Okay, I was embarrassed.

"What should I do?" I asked.

"Go to Bloomingdale's," Jenny said. "Buy some designer jeans that fit. Get a couple of designer shirts and a pair of shoes too."

Okay, I was going to go to Bloomingdale's.

I was looking in Bloomingdale's jeans section, and I was in shock—sticker shock! I had only worn Levi's, which were about fifty bucks, but some of these were $200 a pair! Okay, married guys wore Levi's, single guys wear designer jeans. I started looking through the stacks for my size when a sales clerk came over to me. She was in her late thirties and seemed to have a sense of style in the way she dressed.

"What size are you looking for?" she asked me.

"Thirty-six, waist. Thirty-two, length."

"Okay. What style?"

"Blue."

She looked at me like I had horns out of my head. Then she started laughing.

"Honey, you need some help. Let me pick some out for you to try on. Turn around." She grabbed the material in the back of my comfortable Levi's. "You don't have much of a butt," she said.

And she proceeded to fill her arms with jeans.

I took them to the dressing room and started to try them on. The first pair was Joe's Jeans, and they just felt funny. The second pair looked and felt okay, but a bit tighter than I was used to. These were definitely not relaxed-fit Levi's!

"Are you coming out?" I heard the clerk.

"What?"

"I want to see them on you." So out I went.

"Those are okay, but they aren't great. Try the next pair."

I came back out in the Joe's.

"Oh, no! Take those off!"

I tried on the Hugo Boss and went out.

"Those are keepers. Turn around. Yep, definitely," she said with a smile.

I went out in the next pair.

"Your butt isn't big enough to pull off the horseshoes."

Well, okay. I'm glad I don't have a big butt. I wasn't really into the horseshoes anyway. The next pair felt really good.

"Oh, yeah. Those look fantastic," she said as she was looking at my butt. "The Diesels and the Boss are the best on you."

"Okay, I'll take both. Can you help me with shirts?"

Anyway, I ended up with two Hugo Boss shirts, a Robert Graham shirt, a belt, and a pair of shoes. She said I was definitely leaving with great outfits. Good—I had a date that night. But I couldn't believe I just spent more on this bag of clothes than I spent on my first car.

As I was getting ready for my date, I felt good about the clothes. They were more fitted than what I was used to. I wear suits to work every day and never really had nice casual clothes.

I was driving to pick up Janie, listening to good music and feeling relaxed and confident about my new look. Oops! I forgot to shave. Oh well, too late now. Don't want to be late, and I was almost at her house anyway.

I rang her doorbell. She opened the door and looked at me for a couple of seconds.

"Oh, sweet Jesus, just take me now!" she said.

I guess she liked the outfit. We ended up sending out for Chinese.

The next day, Chris came in my office and asked, "How was your date last night?"

"Pretty good. But what happened to pubic hair?"

"It went out over a decade ago," he stated. "Shaved or a landing strip?"

"Huh?"

"I like it shaved slick."

I had no clue until he explained it to me. And he kept talking.

"Every girl now thinks they want to be a porn star. At thirty-five to forty-five, unmarried, with or without kids, they'd just as soon give you a blow job as shake your hand. And it's expected that you have sex by your third date."

Wow, things had changed. Good to know.

Jenny asked about what I bought, and I told her the story. She liked the shopping part, but not the evening—even though she laughed. She always was my voice of reason.

Would I see Janie again? Probably not.

Next.

CHEAPSKATE

Being just divorced, my bank account balance was well below my comfort level. I had no furniture, no dishes, no silverware, nothing. It was sad walking into my empty house.

Saving money for my house was a priority, and furniture is expensive! So is dating. I don't think most women appreciate what guys do in making plans and paying for everything. I know it's what a gentleman is supposed to do, but I think most women just take it for granted. Will she like the place? Will she like the wine? Is there room on my credit card for dinner?

I met Toni through a friend, and we made plans to go out. I didn't have much money, and I had a date before payday. I went online looking for deals, and I found a Groupon for a restaurant I wanted to try.

Toni and I met there. The restaurant had a nice interior vibe. We talked and got to know each other. Dinner went well. We talked about all of the usual things. She seemed interesting.

The evening was wrapping up, and the server brought the check. I pulled out my credit card and the Groupon coupon I printed off the Internet.

A few minutes, later the server brought the receipt back.

"I deducted the coupon from your check, and the gratuity was added to your check as it said on the coupon," the server said.

"Thank you," I replied.

Toni looked at me. "You used a coupon on me?" she asked. "I'm not good enough to go full price?"

"No! This was a restaurant I wanted to try, and you said you did too. The fact that I found a coupon that saved $42.50 makes it better," I said.

We went outside, and I walked her to her car.

"Can I see you again?" I asked her.

"No. I don't date cheapskates."

Okay, I get it—coupons on first dates don't make a great impression. Lesson learned. But was she being narrow-minded or was I? She seemed nice, but this made her seem kind of shallow. I don't know. I could have taken her to a less expensive restaurant and spent the same amount of money, but I thought taking her somewhere nicer would be better even if I did use a coupon.

I meant well and tried to show her a nice time. I guess she didn't appreciate my efforts.

I got paid. And couple weeks later, I was out with Beth. She was a friend of a friend. After talking a few times, we met at a nicer restaurant. When I saw her there, she looked great.

We were seated at a table. I brought a nice bottle of wine from my collection for dinner, and I put in on the table as we were seated.

"Why did you bring that?" she asked.

"You said you liked red wine, so I thought I'd bring something good from my collection. It's an eight-year-old bottle of Rubicon Cabernet. It should be great by now," I told her.

"Why don't you just order one off the menu?"

"Their wine menu is decent, but there's nothing on it that's aged like the one I brought. If this was on the menu, it would be over $200."

"So you bring your own wine to save money?"

"No. I bring them because my wines are usually better than what they have on the menu. They charge a corkage fee for wines brought in. Most restaurants do it."

"Seems like a lot of trouble just for a bottle of wine," she said.

I guess she didn't know as much about wine as I thought, and now she probably thought I was a cheapskate too. I regretted bringing such a nice bottle to share with her. I should have ordered a bottle of their house wine, and she probably would have been happier.

"Very, very nice wine," the waiter said as he grabbed the bottle and looked at it. "This was a great year, and anything from this area of Napa is good. Would you like me to open it?"

The evening started off on shaky ground, and it never really got any better—conversation was awkward, and there just wasn't any chemistry. By the end of dinner, I liked the wine better than I liked Beth. It was going nowhere.

Well, the waiter understood, but I wasn't going to date him.

Next.

CATHY

My friend Mike was one of about twenty people getting an award, and he invited me to attend the recognition luncheon. I told him I'd be honored to be there. Mike was a coworker, and he had invited his assistant Mary from my office too. Mike left early, and Mary and I rode there together.

The event was at an upscale country club, and there were about forty tables set up. I found Mike's table, which was set up for ten people. Mike reintroduced me to his parents, whom I had met sometime ago, and a couple of his other friends. As the others arrived at the table, we all introduced ourselves.

"Bob, I'd like you to meet Cathy," Mike said.

She was stunning—absolutely beautiful, about five feet five, 120 pounds, long brown hair, and was wearing a great dress and shoes. And she wasn't wearing a wedding ring.

We talked a moment before the program started, and I sat between Mary and Cathy.

Lunch was first, with the presentations after. During lunch, Cathy and I never stopped talking.

"I love a man who knows how to wear a suit," she said as she touched my arm to feel the material. "Italian?" she asked.

"Yes."

Mary leaned over and whispers firmly, "Would you two stop it?"

Several times I had told Mary and my assistant, Jenny, stories of times when women seemed to come onto me, but they always dismissed them. They never believed me. Mary now had a front row seat.

As lunch was wrapping up, for some reason I didn't get a dessert. Cathy asked if I wanted to get a waiter to bring me one. I told her I really only wanted a bite, but I didn't need the calories. She fed me a bite of hers.

"Oh, God, help me," Mary said under her breath as she was rolling her eyes.

During the presentation, Cathy scooted her chair closer to mine and kept touching my arm.

"Would you two stop or get a room?" Mary whispered to me during the program.

I just smiled.

Mike walked onstage to receive his award, and we all clapped and cheered for him.

After it was over, I kept talking to Cathy. I could tell Mary was getting impatient and wanted to get back to the office. I said goodbye to Cathy.

Mary gave me an earful on the ride back. It was funny. And when we got to the office, she walked straight to Jenny's office to give her all the details, play by play.

"See, all those stories I told you were true. Maybe now you'll believe me," I said to them.

"I saw it first hand," Mary replied. "I think I need a shower."

I had a problem. I didn't know how to reach Cathy. I couldn't spell her last name and didn't know where she worked. Later that afternoon, I called Mike. He had her cell number.

I waited a day to call her.

"I really liked meeting you and hoped we could go out sometime," I told her.

"I'd like that a lot."

Over the next few weeks, we went out several times—dinners, happy hour, and a concert. She was beautiful, professional, smart, interesting, and we definitely had chemistry.

Then the call.

"I can't go out with you on Saturday," she said.

"All right. Is everything okay?"

"Well, my on-again, off-again relationship with another guy is kind of back on."

I was really disappointed.

Over the next year or so, she would call me and say they were off again, and we would go out a few times. Then they'd get back together. After the second time that happened, I told her I wasn't playing that game anymore. It was like she couldn't stand to not have a boyfriend, and I was her backup.

It's a shame. She had a lot of potential, and there seemed to be chemistry. With all of her great qualities, I learned she was a bit of a flake and somewhat insecure.

Six months later, she called me.

"My best friend just moved here, and I told her you are a really great guy. I thought you may like to meet her—she's really a lot of fun," she said.

It was like she realized I was a good catch, and if she wasn't going to get me, she'd set me up with her best friend. I was flattered, but no.

"No, thanks, Cathy. I'm good."

Next.

TURKEY

Shannon sent me a message saying she liked my profile. She had an interesting profile herself. She seemed a bit eclectic—lots of different interests, fun pictures, seemed light-hearted, and a bit of a free spirit.

Talking with her, she was a little quirky but funny. We decided to meet for brunch on Sunday. It was a beautiful day, so I got a table outside while I waited for her to arrive. I saw a pickup truck drive up and park, and she got out. She had stickers on the back, like "Got Mud?" "Save a Horse, Ride a Cowboy," "PETA— People Eating Tasty Animals," and "Fat-Bottomed Girls Rule."

Uh oh. What had I gotten myself into?

Her outfit had some Cyndi Lauper touches with a splash of Madonna overlaying a definite redneck base. There was a feather woven into her hair. And her bottom was, well, fully developed and then some; and she had the bumper sticker to back it up.

As we sat and ate, the conversation was all over the place. Shannon was definitely amusing.

She was telling me a story about the cute things her lap dog does. Then she was telling me about the time she met Stevie Nicks. Then she pulled out her phone and showed me a picture of her dog and of her and Stevie.

She told me about when she took her nieces and nephews to Disney World. Then I saw pictures of them with Disney characters. There was even a picture of her nephew's bloody mouth after she pulled his loose tooth before they went on Pirates of the Caribbean.

She told me all about a bachelorette party she went to Friday night, how wasted everyone was at the male revue, how some of them were topless somewhere—and yes, she had pictures of all of it. She even had a picture of the bride-to-be right after she puked.

"What other pictures do you have on that?" I asked.

"Here's one of the fourteen stitches I had when I cut my hand."

"How did you do that?"

"I did it cutting a steak at Longhorn's."

"How did you do that?"

"Oh, it's a skill. I make being a klutz an art form."

She was scrolling through her pictures, looking for more to share with me.

"What's that a picture of?"

"My vibrator," she replied matter-of-factly.

Of course I had to ask, "Why do you have a picture of your vibrator?"

"Why not?"

Good point.

She was entertaining, but not my type.

"Want to see a picture of the turkey I shot?"

"Hey, Jenny, what are you doing for Thanksgiving?"

Next.

SOMEBODY'S MOM

Donna and I had messaged each other a few times, and I learned that she worked downtown, not too far from my office. Her profile was interesting, with us sharing a lot of common interests. She had several pictures posted, and she was attractive. We talked one time by phone, and things went okay. She suggested we meet.

I usually don't meet with someone after only one call. I try to learn more about them before I go the time, and usually the expense, of meeting someone. What do they sound like? Do they talk correctly? Are they boring? Do they seem like a wacko? If we can't seem to start some sort of connection or have poor interaction on the phone, how are we going to in person?

What the heck, she worked close to me, what would it hurt? I told her I was busy, but I agreed to meet Donna at Starbucks the next day.

My dad used to tell me if you're five minutes early, you're on time; if you're there on time, you're late; and if you're late, you're fired. So I arrived a few minutes early as usual. I was sitting in a chair watching people come and go, keeping an eye for Donna.

A woman I noticed ordered a coffee, and then came over to me.

"Hi, I'm Donna."

And I was floored! She didn't look anything like her picture. In fact, I could hardly recognize any resemblance to the pictures she had posted. Those pictures had to be at least ten years old, and probably twenty pounds ago. I was expecting who I saw in the pictures—who was this woman? Okay, okay, think, quickly! Say something!

"Hi. It's nice to meet you. Please, sit down."

I wanted to say "When is your daughter getting here?" but I was a gentleman and not a smart-ass.

And we started to chat. She tried to carry on a conversation, but I was disengaged. I couldn't get over how different she was from her pictures. On her Match.com profile, I thought she looked good, but in person, she was at least ten years older than she said. Her pictures showed a slender woman; this woman was not slender. I felt duped. I remembered what Chris said—that some are not always honest online. He was right.

I thought about confronting her about it, but I didn't. What would it really accomplish? It would just upset her in some way; there was no need. She must have known she didn't look like her pictures anymore, and I think her age had been fudged more than just a little. Why do people do that?

Maybe she was delusional. I guess they think they can get away with it. Maybe I should have asked her about it. Are some people that insecure or desperate that they have to lie about who they are?

If someone is trying to meet people with the possibility of developing a relationship, wouldn't they want it to start out being honest? How can a lasting relationship be built when there are lies from the start? If she was lying about things in the beginning, what else would she lie about? How could I trust her? Maybe I'm just naïve or idealistic. But I know what I stand for and what I want in a woman. This was not it.

After about fifteen minutes, I politely excused myself saying I had to get back to work. She asked if we could get together again, and I told her I didn't think so. I could see the disappointment on her face. I felt sorry for her. I wonder if she saw the surprised amazement on mine when she walked up to me.

When I got back to my office, I checked her profile again online to see if I had made a mistake. I saw her profile. I was right. The pictures could have been her daughter.

That's it! Dang! I should have asked if she had a daughter!

(Note to self: In the future, ask how old their pictures are.)

I got back to the office, and I told Jenny what just happened. She couldn't believe it either. And she told me to stay away from the daughters—probably good advice.

This dating thing looked like it may be more difficult than I thought.

Jenny just laughed.

Next.

OLIVE GARDEN

Mandy and I worked together and had been friends for several years. We kind of flirted a little bit, but nothing was going to happen—she was about twenty years younger than me. I really liked Mandy. She was so sweet and cute. I wanted to set her up with my son, but he was too young, and I was too old.

She and I were both Florida State football fans, and they were coming to town to play in a bowl game. I asked Mandy if she wanted some tickets.

"Of course!" she replied. "How many can I have?"

I didn't tell her how many I had.

"If I give you four, will you think I'm a great guy?"

"I already think you're a great guy! Four would be fantastic! I have some girlfriends I'll invite."

"I have tickets to a pregame hospitality tent too for all of you."

"You rock!"

The day of the game, my son and I were in the hospitality tent, having a beer and some barbecue and talking to some friends. I also talked with some clients

I had given tickets to, and they were having a good time and thanked me for the tickets.

About that time, Mandy and her friends came into the tent, and everyone's eyes shifted to them. Well, at least every guy. There were four beautiful women in their late twenties dressed up for a game—tight jeans, tight shirts, heels, push-up bras. Wow!

They came over to me and my son. Mandy hugged us, and they all thanked me for the tickets. My son and I got them beers while they got some food, and we sat together.

The girls were all nice. We all talked and got to know each other a little. Christie sat by me. She seemed a little older than the other girls—maybe early thirties. And she was pretty—long wavy brown hair and a twinkle in her eye.

The girls all hugged me before we went to the game. Their seats weren't close to us, so we went our own ways.

The next day, Mandy came into my office.

"Thanks again for the tickets. The seats were great! And the barbecue was good—and free beer! Thank you so much. We all had a great time."

"You're welcome."

"Christie thought you were cool too."

"I am!" I said as I laughed.

"Oh, okay, Mr. Hot Stuff," she laughed. "She hopes you call her." And she gave me Christie's number.

A couple of days later, I called Christie. She thanked me for the tickets and said she was glad Mandy invited her. And she was glad she met me. We talked for a while and made plans to meet for lunch.

I wasn't sure about lunch. She was a CPA with a big firm, but she was young! I went to meet her with an open mind.

I told Jenny what happened and that I was meeting Mandy's friend for lunch.

"Cradle robber!" she called me. "You know you shouldn't do it. She's one of Mandy's friends, for God's sake!"

"It's just lunch," I told her.

"I'm telling you, it's not going to work out—you're too old for her!"

"I'm not old!"

"You are for her," she laughed.

When I met Christie, she was dressed very professionally in a skirt and blouse—quite a bit different from how she looked at the game.

The conversation was going well. I was afraid there would be a big generation gap or some awkwardness with our conversation due to age and different interests and experiences—not to mention maturity. But it was going surprisingly better than I expected.

I really wanted to know how old she was, but I couldn't ask her. I told her one of my kids was having a birthday in a couple of weeks, and she said her birthday was next week. Well, I wasn't going to ask what birthday it was, and I wasn't going to commit to taking her out for her birthday either.

"What are you doing for your birthday?"

"Oh, I am going out with a bunch of girlfriends. Probably go to some clubs downtown."

"What's your favorite restaurant?" I asked her.

"Favorite?"

"Yeah. If you could pick a restaurant, where would you go for your birthday dinner?"

"Olive Garden," she said.

Olive Garden? That's my twelve-year-old daughter's favorite restaurant! She might as well have said Chuck E Cheese. There were plenty of very nice, upscale restaurants in the area, and she picks Olive Garden. There's nothing wrong with Olive Garden, but it's not what I consider a special occasion restaurant.

I didn't take her out for her birthday. I let her girlfriends do that. She must have been younger than I thought—or less mature than I thought. Mandy later told me it was Christie's twenty-eighth birthday.

Christie was a sweet girl. With the Olive Garden comment, she became my daughter.

I wonder what her mom looks like.

I wasn't telling Mandy.

I did tell Jenny, and she laughed and said, "Told you so!"

I hate when she tells me that! And I hate when she's right.

Next.

PSYCHIC

Janie's profile was interesting. She was thirty-eight with a lot of varied interests. Oh, yeah, and she was very attractive.

She worked downtown not too far from me, so we met for a glass of wine after work one day. I had talked to her on the phone once or twice before we met, and things went okay. When I met her in the wine bar, she started talking.

"Where did you grow up?" she started.

"Central—"

"I grew up outside Atlanta. Have you ever been to Atlanta? I love it there. I graduated from UNC Chapel Hill. Where did you go?"

"Florida St—"

"I am so glad I moved to Florida. I love the beach. Do you like the beach? There's a woman in my office who doesn't like the beach. Have you ever heard of something so ridiculous? Who doesn't like the beach?"

"Well, I—"

"I know you like the beach from your profile. We should go to the beach together. I really want to go to Hawaii someday. I love listening to country music at the beach. I could listen to Toby Keith all the time. Some of his songs are sooo funny! Don't you think so?"

"I like—"

"Sounds like you have a great job. Mine is pretty good, but the drama some of the people in my office create is unbelievable! Oh my god! The things they talk about and complain about! And you should see what they post on Facebook! None of them are in happy relationships. And the affairs! The lady in the cubicle next to mine—everyone thinks her husband abuses her. Yep. And we just found out my supervisor's kid had a meth lab in their pool house. I heard their dog got into it and died. Can you believe it?"

No, I was having a hard time believing the whole situation. I felt like I was being abused. Her hotness was long gone.

"One lady's son is serving in Iraq, and his baby mama is living with her and working as a stripper—on poles and everything. The baby mama hangs out with a drag queen. And damn if he doesn't look better than most women! I've seen the pictures on Facebook. I swear, you'd think some of those people were in Jerry Springer auditions! I saw a Groupon for pole dancing lessons that looked like fun."

I felt like I was in a Jerry Springer audition myself. Maybe I should start praying.

"So you have three kids? I have two, and they are such a handful! Joey plays soccer, and Liza plays volleyball. I am always taking them someplace. Let me show you their pictures."

I bet her kids wished they were involved in more activities to get away from listening to their mom. Okay, I'm almost done with this glass of wine. I have to get out of here without being rude. Where's the waitress so I can get the check?

"And they are sooo smart. Joey was tested for gifted, but he didn't make it. He's just too easily distracted. I think he's ADHD. I ought to get him checked for it. And Liza just made the honor roll. I think they get their smarts from my dad's side—he was really smart. They sure didn't get it from their father! Hahahaha!"

By this time, I thought I was listening to Charlie Brown's teacher: whah whah whah whah whah. I was looking around to see where Jerry's film crew was. Was I being punked? I think I'm getting a headache. No, I am sure I'm getting a headache.

I interrupted her to let her know I had to pick up one of my kids from one of their activities and needed to get going.

"Oh, I totally understand. It was sooo nice meeting you. We had such a good conversation! You are sooo interesting, like a tall, dark, handsome man of mystery. I really had a good time. I can't wait to see you again. Tomorrow, I'm going to see a psychic, and I'm going to ask her what we may have in our future."

Okay, you do that, but I could have saved her what a fortune teller charges for a reading. I didn't need to see a psychic to know there was no future for me with this woman. I knew why she was single. But I believe there is someone out there for everyone, and she had to be around a man long enough to get knocked up—twice. Did she talk like that while they were . . . nope, not going there. Just walk away—cleanly.

Maybe she should put in her profile that she's looking for a man with severe hearing difficulties.

The next day in the office, Jenny asked how my date was.

I just didn't feel like talking—or listening.

Next.

GOING TO VEGAS

I ran into Elaine at my high school reunion. I really didn't know her well when we were in school. She was a cheerleader in high school, and she still had a great figure. She hadn't changed much. (I can't say that for everyone I saw there! What I can say is thank goodness for name tags.)

I said hello to her. "Why didn't we know each other better in high school?" I asked her.

"I don't know. I was kind of new to school and really didn't know a lot of people back then. I guess I was kind of shallow then too."

We talked for a few minutes, and we both drifted into other groups. I kept mingling in the crowd, visiting and reconnecting with old friends, reliving the past and telling favorites stories from back in the day. I hadn't gone to the last couple of class reunions, and now I wish I had.

While circulating through the room, I ran into Elaine again. The DJ played a great song from our era, and I grabbed her hand and took her to the dance floor without saying a word. Afterward, we got a drink at the bar and started talking more.

She said she had been divorced about five years and had a son who just graduated from high school.

She was a middle school teacher and lived about three hours away. She said she had family living in my city and visited them fairly often. I told her I'd like to see her the next time she was in town.

We talked several times over the next few weeks. She told me what weekend she was going to be in town, and we made plans to meet.

I picked her up at her relatives' place, and she looked fantastic—sexy dress, sexy woman. We had a great time at dinner. The food was great, wine was great, and conversation was great.

After dinner, we went to a wine bar and listened to pretty good live music. She told me several times that she was enjoying herself, and she reached to hold my hand.

"I wish we didn't live so far apart," she said.

The conversation continued; the wine continued to flow. She was interesting. We kissed a few times. It was a great date.

We talked about not being out late since she was staying with relatives, especially in case they may stay up waiting to let her in, so I started to take her home.

"I'd like to see you again," I told her.

"I'd like that a lot. I really had a great time."

"What does your schedule look like the next couple weekends?"

"Well, next Thursday I'm going to Las Vegas and L.A. with my ex-boyfriend, and we won't be back until the following weekend. He has a couple of conventions. But we could get together when I get back."

What? She's going with her ex-boyfriend? It didn't seem like an ex if they were going to be together on a trip for about ten days.

"I thought you weren't seeing anyone?" I asked.

"No, I'm not. We're just friends."

"That seems odd to me that you would do that with an ex."

"I love to travel, and I love Vegas!" She was excited about the trip.

An ex-boyfriend you travel across the country with? Did I really think they were getting separate rooms? I might have fallen off the turnip truck, but I didn't fall off yesterday. I had a great time, but I wasn't going to see someone who was dating me while she's involved with someone else. Guess I'm a bit old fashioned. By that time, I was disengaged and started driving her home faster.

I don't know exactly what I was feeling at that point. Surprised. Disappointed. Duped. It was definitely a letdown. I thought she was pretty and interesting and had potential. Wow. You never know.

Trying to maintain my civility and being a gentleman, I walked her to the doorstep. Elaine again told me that she had a great time and looked forward to seeing me again. She'd let me know when she got back. I told her good night. So much potential; such a disappointment.

I didn't hear from Elaine at all while she was on her trip. A couple of weeks later, she texted me that she was back and for me to call her when I had a chance.

All I could think about was the Jimmy Buffet song, "If the Phone Doesn't Ring, It's Me."

Next.

SATURDAY VISIT

Debra had a fairly plain vanilla profile, but her eyes and smile attracted my attention. I talked to her a couple of times. She seemed nice, so I agreed to meet her at a restaurant next to my office on a Thursday.

I was having a busy day at work when my Outlook calendar reminder popped up about my lunch date. I had fifteen minutes to get there. If I had more time, I would have cancelled, and doing so would be rude. I had so much work to do, but on I went. I hate to be stood up, and I wasn't going to do it to someone else.

We got to the hostess stand at the same time. Debra had a pretty face, but she was much heavier than I expected. Her picture was obviously taken a few years and more than a couple of pounds ago.

On the Match.com profiles, people put their body type in their profile—athletic, slender, average, a few extra pounds, curvy, etc. Her profile said she was average. When did average start to mean twenty pounds overweight? I guess it's all perspective.

We sat and talked. My mind was elsewhere. I hate to seem shallow, but she wasn't really what I was looking for physically, and I had work waiting for me. I was basically going through the motions with idle chit chat. My salad was good, though.

Lunch ended. Debra said she hoped I would call again as we went our own ways.

I worked hard the rest of the day and had pretty much forgotten about Debra.

Saturday morning, I had just gotten out of the shower after taking a twenty-mile bike ride when the doorbell rang. I put on some shorts and a T-shirt to answer the door. It was Debra.

"Hello," I said as I opened the door.

"Hi! I was just in the neighborhood, and I thought I'd stop by," she said.

I was shocked. I live in a somewhat rural suburb—she lived about twenty miles away.

"How did you find me?"

"I went to the county property tax website and found your address there. I also found it on whitepages.com."

Okay. Now I was a little freaked out. She was a stalker.

"I wish you hadn't come by."

"What are you doing today?" she asked.

"I have a full day planned. And I'm sorry, but I really don't want you coming here again."

"Really? Okay. I just thought I'd take a chance. Bye."

She took a chance of getting shot—or dealing with the cops. The nerve! There are other ways to get my attention and be bold. Maybe I was overreacting. I wasn't interested in her, and I didn't want to deal with a wacko. All I could think of was Glenn Close in Fatal Attraction. I started making sure my doors were locked at night. I never saw her again, thankfully.

Jenny and Mandy couldn't believe it. I had a hard time believing it myself.

Next.

PANTIES IN MY POCKET

As with many business jobs, a lot of what I do is business development. The best way to develop business is through referrals, and the best referrals come through centers of influence. So I go to lunch and drinks after work often with attorneys and CPAs.

One day, I was meeting three attorneys for lunch at a nice restaurant four or five blocks from my office. The senior partner was a man about my age, the junior partner was a guy about thirty-five, and the third was a kind of attractive female junior associate, maybe thirty, Jill.

Lunch went well. Conversation about business was very good; there were definite business opportunities for me and their law firm. We were doing some brainstorming, coming up with good ideas. Jill, who was sitting on my right, didn't talk much. She seemed to bump my leg with her foot a few times. I thought nothing of it. Every time I looked at her, she was smiling at me.

As the check came, we exchanged business cards, and then Jill excused herself—we all had a lot of iced tea. We headed out as she returned. Outside the restaurant, we were wrapping up everything with things to follow up and calls to make. I noticed Jill behind me saying hi to some girlfriends at the outside tables.

The sidewalk was very narrow, with a four-foot-high railing between the sidewalk and the outdoor dining area. A big crowd of people was coming by, and we all kind of leaned against the railing to make room for them. I felt Jill leaning against my back shoulder. After the crowd passed, we said our goodbyes and headed back to work.

As I was walking back to my office, my phone chimed. I had received a text.

"Check your coat pocket. Jill." She had my cell number from my business card.

I reached into my pocket, what the . . . I pulled out a pair of red lace and satin panties, sized small. I couldn't believe it! She must have slipped them into my pocket when the crowd passed. What kind of girl does that? Did she take them off in the ladies' room or did she have an extra pair in her purse?

I get back to my office and go into my friend Mark's office to tell him what just happened. Mark has been married about twenty-five years. He doesn't believe my story. Then, I pulled the panties out of my pocket and threw them on his desk. You would have thought he saw a ghost—his jaw dropped, his mouth was wide open, and his eyes were about to bulge out of his head.

"Get those out of here!" he demanded.

Mark and I talked about the meeting; he wanted all the details of how it happened. We had a good laugh about it.

"You seem to attract that kind of woman," he said.

"What is that supposed to mean?"

"You know."

Jenny walked in, and I relived it with her. Mark was just smiling.

"I can't believe it," she said.

"Believe it." And I showed her the panties.

"Oh my god!" And she walked back to her office, talking to herself and shaking her head.

I put the panties into a locked Iron Mountain shred box. I wondered what the guy thought when he discovered them in the box and had to shred them.

A few minutes later, Mandy came into my office with a big grin on her face. Jenny must have told her.

"Soooo, how was your lunch?" she asked.

I never replied to Amanda, and I never replied to Jill's text. The next day, she called.

"I'm so sorry! I've never done anything like that before! I'm so embarrassed!" she said.

"Don't worry about it. We all do things we regret. It's okay."

"Thank you for understanding."

"No problem," I replied, but I really didn't understand.

"Want to get together sometime?"

Maybe I should introduce her to Chris. No, he probably already knows her.

Next.

YOU LIKE WHAT?

Valerie's profile told the story of a divorced mom who was working to support her son—nothing really special or interesting, just normal. She looked attractive in her pictures. I reached out to her, and we started messaging and talking.

She had a sweet voice. I learned quickly that she was a caring mother, went to church, and really didn't have much of a social life. That's why she joined Match.com. We agreed to meet for lunch.

I waited for her at the restaurant entrance, and she walked in. Her pictures were accurate; she was about five feet seven, slender, with straight blonde hair just past her shoulders, and she had beautiful big brown eyes.

We talked about our kids. Her son was thirteen years old and very active in sports, especially soccer. He seemed like a good kid; she was obviously proud of him, as she should be.

We talked about my kids too and shared parenting stories. I have a son several years older than hers who had tried my patience a few times and challenged my parenting skills more than once.

So I shared a few experiences I had with him to kind of give her an idea of what to possibly expect.

Although, I told her that her son would probably never try some of the pranks my son did. She laughed at the stories.

And we talked about our jobs. It was a very natural, smooth conversation—not the awkward exchange first meetings can be. Valerie really seemed like a caring, sweet woman and a good mom.

We were finishing lunch, talking about a soccer tournament her son was going to be in this weekend, when she asked, "Do you like anal sex?"

I just about choked! Did she really just ask that?

"I'm kind of kinky that way," she deadpanned, so matter-of-factly.

"Oh, okay." It was all I could get out.

What the heck was I supposed to say to that? My mind was all over the place. Did she mean giving or receiving? I suddenly wasn't hungry. This seemingly sweet woman had a fetish she felt she had to get out there on the first date, like it would be a deal breaker for her.

I wasn't being judgmental, and I have an open mind. But anyone who would bring that up while on a first date, let alone while eating, made it a deal breaker for me. I guess I was hoping for a little more class. At least some subtlety—there is a time and place for about everything, I think.

Then, Valerie was back to talking about something going on at her job. She didn't skip a beat.

A few minutes later, she asked, "Want to go to church with me sometime?"

Oh, those soccer moms.

"How was lunch?" Jenny asked.

I told her.

"Eewww!"

Next.

NURSE DIVA

Felicia's picture caught my eye. She was very pretty; another blue-eyed blonde with a very pretty face. We messaged back and forth several times, but we never actually talked until we met. I knew that wasn't very smart, but I was going to be in her area, so I thought, what the heck. Plus, she was hot. She lived about forty-five minutes away.

She lived in a relatively small town, and she picked a wine bar on Main Street for us to meet. It was kind of dingy. I looked at the wine list before she arrived, and the most expensive bottle was $35. I could afford to be a big spender here!

She arrived, and her pictures did her little justice—she was a knockout. And when she talked, she had a soft West Virginia accent that melted me. She started talking about how excited she was about taking her three-year-old grandson to Disney the coming weekend.

Grandson! She must have started when she was fourteen! Well, she was from West Virginia.

Wait a second. When did I go from MILFs to GILFs? I'm too young to be a grandfather! Yep, I didn't see that one coming.

She asked a lot of questions but made it conversational—kids, job, house, travel, the usual. I commented, "You have a lot of questions."

She replied, "I want to learn about you. I am very, very choosy."

I guess I was passing because we ordered another glass of wine and appetizers. She talked about her job. She had been a nurse for a while but recently became a nurse anesthetist at the local hospital. I knew very little about that field.

She said she made about $125,000 a year. Wow! I had no idea nurses made that kind of money. With me being in the financial field, I told her, "I hope you're saving some of it."

"No, not really," she said.

"What about retirement?" I asked.

"I guess I'll have to worry about it sometime."

"What do you do with all your money?"

"I like to go on cruises and take my family. I buy things. I re-did my kitchen."

"You must buy a lot of things."

"Well, I'm kind of not very good with money."

"What do you mean?"

"I just got a letter that they're going to foreclose on my house. My car is paid up to date, but the student loan people keep calling me for a payment."

"How long has it been since you made a student loan payment?"

"I've never made one."

"How long ago did you graduate?"

"Two years ago."

"Have you made *any* payments on it?"

"Nope."

"They can take your tax refund and ruin your credit for that kind of stuff."

"That must be why I didn't get my tax refund! Dammit!"

"Why is the house being foreclosed?"

"I heard the government was forcing banks to work with people, so I stopped paying."

"Why don't you catch the payments up? I'm sure they'd rather have you do that rather than foreclose on you."

"Yeah, I guess so, but I don't have any money to catch it up. I have a lot of legal bills too."

"What are the legal bills for?"

"I got arrested for a domestic incident with my ex-husband, and I'm paying for my son's divorce."

"What kind of incident?

"Well, you know, I was home, drinking. Then I found out he was coming home after seeing his mistress, so I broke a picture frame over his head."

I feel it. Jerry's film crew must be in the area.

"Yeah, the glass broke and cut my hand, and I needed stitches. He did too, but he deserved it."

"What about your son?"

"I didn't like his wife, so I'm paying for his divorce."

"So what are you going to do?"

"I don't know. You're the financial guy."

Was she asking me questions about my job and stuff to see if I could bail her out? Too much baggage here. Check, please!

Some women come with a high price—she came with high, past due balances.

She went from being hot to a hot mess to just a mess.

I told Jenny and Mandy to make sure they were participating in the 401(k) plan because I wasn't going to bail them out.

Next.

VELVET SESSIONS

When I first started talking with Scarlett, I was quite intrigued. She was witty, charming, and flirtatious. She was educated, a corporate professional, pretty in her pictures, and had a lot of common interests with me. She had been a college football cheerleader and sounded like she was full of positive energy. She said she liked my frat boy voice. Plus, she not only liked wine—she knew a lot about it. Finally, we agreed to meet for a glass of wine at a restaurant.

I got to the restaurant a few minutes early and ordered. Knowing she liked wine, I brought a bottle of Chateau Ste Michelle Artist Series Meritage to give Scarlett. It's a pretty good wine. She came in and looked just like in her pictures. She dressed great and was wearing some shoes with Swarovski crystals, she later told me. She was pretty but, even more, she seemed to have a cool confidence, which made her more attractive. I welcomed her with a hug, and she took the barstool next to me.

"What are you drinking?" she asked.

"Far Niente Chardonnay."

"I'll have a glass of that too," she said to the bartender. And she began to talk about a trip she had to Napa.

I reached down the floor, retrieved the wine bag, and gave her the bottle—and she was impressed. Then she surprised me—she gave me a bottle! Rafanelli Zinfandel is pretty much only available from the winery. Okay, she definitely had my attention.

We had a great conversation; everything clicked. Halfway through our second glass, Scarlett mentioned Velvet Sessions was starting in forty-five minutes and Little River Band was playing. I asked her if she wanted to go. We were off.

During the slower summer months, the Hard Rock hotel has a concert series on Thursday nights with bands pretty much from the 1980s. It's an interesting crowd of about five hundred—seems like there are groups of women, guys on the prowl, and couples.

We walked in with enough time to get another glass of wine and ran into some of her girlfriends before the show started. The band members looked like they were well into their late fifties and early sixties. One was almost bald, but they sounded great! I had forgotten how many hit songs they had.

Scarlett and I were kind of dancing to the music when we caught each other's eye, and we kissed. And we kept kissing—I think through most of the rest of the concert. She was a good kisser! She kissed like I liked! She said she liked the way I kissed. (Ever notice how everyone thinks they are a good kisser? Kind of like women thinking they have great breasts, just because they have breasts!)

The concert ended, and we said goodbye to her friends. She suggested we get one more glass of wine while the crowds exited. There would probably be at least a thirty-minute wait at the parking valet.

In the lounge, we found a couch in the corner and started kissing again. Trying to hide some of the embarrassment, we both joked about the cocktail waitress who interrupted us for me to pay for the wine. We were making out like school kids—in public. I guess I had too much wine.

It was getting late. I had to work the next day, so we called it a night. We would see each other several times later, but it just didn't work out. I learned with her that good chemistry is important, but timing is critical.

Later, I told Jenny that I wasn't seeing Scarlett anymore.

"Shame. You let a good one get away," she told me.

She was right. Jenny was usually right. I hate that.

Next.

CHURCH LADY NUMBER 1

I came across Sharon as someone with interests similar to mine—like over a ninety percent match. I'm not sure how we were paired since I was looking for someone within fifteen miles of my house, but she lived about an hour away.

Like Barney on *How I Met Your Mother* might say, "I never date anyone who lives far away, wait for it, unless she's hot." And she was very attractive, with long blonde hair.

Sharon said she was very active in her church, singing in the choir and in a praise band. When we started talking, I could tell she was a bit forceful—not really pushy, but a little aggressive, like she was a go-getter. She seemed nice. But she did live an hour away!

After a week or two of talking, she invited me over for dinner. I told her to pick a restaurant where we could meet. She picked the fanciest, most expensive restaurant in town. I was okay with it, but did find it a bit presumptuous for a first date. I like fine dining and fine wines, so I went with it.

We met, and she was prettier than in her pictures. She was wearing a black cocktail dress, low-cut and slit up the side. She ordered a dirty martini while we waited for a bottle of wine. This was not what I was expecting from a church lady.

Dinner conversation was good, but at times I felt as if we were dancing and she was trying to lead. We talked about her family up north, her job at NASA, and her church and singing. She reached for my hand a few times, and I obliged. Later, she started to rub my leg with her foot. She was nice, pretty, interesting, but her pushiness tended to extinguish any potential spark.

After dinner, we walked around outside the restaurant in the town village in the dark, just window shopping and talking. I liked looking in the antique shops and art galleries. We got close to where she parked, and I walked her to her car.

We were saying our goodbyes when she reached up to kiss me. I like kissing, so I kissed her back. She was left breathless—and it's not just my ego. She said that was the most passionate kiss she had in a long time. I thought it was just a kiss.

She came back for more. She pulled me into her. Then she grabbed my package right there in the parking lot. She crouched down and started to pull at my zipper, and I backed away. I knew she was a bit aggressive, but this girl was just downright brazenly bold and horny!

"I really give good head," said the church lady.

I had no doubt. And that was like no church lady like I ever knew. She was a church slut who needed to pay attention in church!

I told her I needed to get home since I had to work the next morning. She invited me to stay at her house and leave in the morning. She practically begged me. I've read the Bible, and I know there are things in there that talk against what she wanted to do! I politely declined.

She said she had so much bottled-up passion. I guess I seemed to have triggered her countdown to blastoff. This was not the Church Lady from *Saturday Night Live.*

What did they preach at her church?

Jenny and I agreed that our churches probably taught different things from hers.

Next.

POOL FIASCO

Shauna was a sexy flight attendant, about forty years old. We had previously met for a lunch and dinner in the last week or so, and she had invited me over to her place Sunday afternoon to hang out at her condo's pool. She said she liked to hang out by the pool because there was usually a fun crowd out there— the partyers were there on Saturdays and a mellower crowd on Sundays. It sounded like fun, so I went.

She lived in a more upscale condo downtown. Her condo was very well-decorated, and Shauna greeted me in her bikini. She was very well-built. She made a few snacks for us to eat before going to the pool, and she was making frozen margaritas for us to take out. I liked how she rubbed up against me a few times, so we were a little delayed in getting sun.

When we finally made it out there, it was a beautiful day. There was not a big crowd, but the people who were there were having fun and playing good music. We talked, listened to music, and enjoyed the warm sunny day. We got into the pool when we got hot. It was nice.

After a few hours out there, she checked her phone after it made a noise. She told me I needed to get going because her husband was on his way home.

What! She was married? And dating? I believe in marriage, and I never want to get in the way of one.

I couldn't have gotten out of there fast enough. All I could think of was Charlie Sheen diving out a bedroom window as some husband walked through the door.

I left and never looked back.

The next day, she texted me to see when we could get together again.

Delete.

I never thought I'd have to ask if someone who wanted to date me was married.

I didn't tell Jenny—no way.

Next.

CATHY'S FRIEND

"Hi, Madelyn, this is Bob from Match. How are you?" I asked on my first call to her.

"I'm good, but having twelve kids at home really wears you out. Especially when you live on a farm," she replied.

"Twelve kids, wow. It reminds me of what Groucho Marx said a long time ago—'I really like my cigar, but I pull it out once in a while'!"

She burst out laughing.

"That's probably the best response I've ever had!" she said.

"How was I supposed to respond?"

"Some guys hang up!" she said. "Some take me seriously and ask questions. It's hilarious."

She really had two grown kids and lived alone in a condo. Her farm was an herb garden in pots on her balcony.

We had a great conversation and arranged to meet at lunch a few days later.

When she walked into the restaurant, I recognized her, but there was something different. It was like her pictures online were five-year-old Glamour Shots pictures where she looked much better. In real life, she was not as attractive and a few pounds heavier than I was expecting.

She definitely had personality, though. And she knew a lot of people in town that could have helped my business.

Madelyn said she recently moved back to the area. She said her best friend, Cathy, would come and see her a lot, and they were both glad they now lived five minutes apart instead of hours.

"I have a friend named Cathy who used to visit a friend where you just moved from," I told her.

After talking further, we found out it was the same Cathy. So this was the Madelyn that Cathy wanted to set me up with.

"I remember her talking about you," she said. "She really thought you were a great guy. She and her boyfriend are looking for a house."

I really didn't want to talk about Cathy.

Madelyn was much more interested in me than I was in her.

"I am very affectionate and giving to my man," she stated.

I just smiled. I knew I wasn't going to find out. It's like she saw me slipping away, so she tried to sweeten the pot by offering to throw a little action my way to keep me on the hook.

She was very nice, pleasant enough, and had a great sense of humor. But physically, she did nothing for me. As we wrapped up lunch, I think she could tell I wasn't interested in seeing her again.

I heard she was married about a year later. Good for her.

She was definitely no Cathy.

Next.

RUSSIAN WEDDING

A friend of mine had been divorced about four years, and at age fifty, he was lonely. No wonder—Greg was a slob. He spent a lot of money on clothes, but he didn't know how to wear them. He would spend $1,500 on a new Italian suit and still look like an unmade bed.

And it didn't stop there. When he ate, you'd think you were sitting in the Shamu Show splash zone. He chewed with his mouth open, made noises when he chewed, and just made a mess—he needed a bib. It was really gross when he burped or had food in his mustache.

I can't believe he was married for almost twenty years.

Even more so, I couldn't believe he found someone that would now marry him.

A few weeks later, I saw Greg out one night and went over to say hello. Greg introduced me to his fiancée, Alana. She was a beautiful! Alana was about thirty-two, around five feet eight, and 130 lbs.—she was a hottie! But she was with Greg! They just didn't match.

She spoke with an Eastern European accent. She excused herself to go to the ladies' room, and Greg told me she was from Russia. They met at a wedding where one of her girlfriends was marrying one of Greg's clients. Greg said the bride seemed like a Russian mail order bride, and many of the wedding goers were Russian women here in the States. Greg said it was like Russian girls are all networked together somehow.

Greg and Alana seemed to have hit it off, and after dating about twelve months, they were engaged. He said it wasn't because she needed a green card, but I wonder what Alana's real motivation was. She was striking, and he was a total slob with few redeeming qualities other than his four golf handicap. I should be supportive, not doubtful or judgmental.

A few months later, I received their wedding announcement.

It was a great day. It was early summer, with clear skies—a perfect day for an outdoor afternoon wedding at his country club.

It was like the wedding Greg described where he met Alana—there were a lot of beautiful women there, and they all had Russian accents. There must have been twenty gorgeous, single, thirty-something-year-old women.

And lucky me, I was just about the only single guy there.

The reception was fun. Great food and wine and a lot of sexy, well-dressed women who were all trying to get my attention—talking to me, asking me to dance, sitting in my lap. I was having a great time! Many of them were getting a bit frisky after a few drinks, and some were not shy about letting me know.

I was sitting while talking to a couple of the women when another woman literally sat on my leg and started to give me a lap dance. Then later the evening went on, the lesser the adjusting of their dresses—dresses riding up, tops not being pulled up, and more cleavage showing.

Greg and Alana were mingling and enjoying themselves, and Greg looked happy. Alana was hanging out and giggling with the girls.

"See any you like?" Greg asked.

"Are you kidding me? I like pretty much all of them!"

"I know. It's like an all you can eat smorgasbord," he said.

Alana came over to us.

"You've made quite an impression on a lot of my friends," Alana told us.

"Really?" I replied. "You have a lot of beautiful friends."

"And they like you," she said. "Go have fun!"

"I am."

"They know how to please a man," she stated.

"I'll vouch for that!" Greg added, laughing, with some cake icing in his mustache.

I wandered back to a group of them. I bet I could have taken home that night my choice of a dozen of them. It was like fishing in a barrel.

Marla had strawberry blonde hair and was wearing a sexy emerald green silk dress—she was hot. Steph was taller, with jet black hair with bangs, and she was wearing an incredible black dress, low-cut and tight— she was hot. Tina was blonde, in a royal blue dress that really set off her blue eyes—and she was hot too.

They were all affectionate and trying to get my undivided attention.

"So you like one of us?" Steph asked with her accent.

"I like all of you!"

"You no have all of us," she laughed.

"I know! It's a shame."

I had three women, each beautiful in their own unique way. They wanted to know which one of them I wanted. I must have been dreaming.

The reception was winding down. Marla said she was staying at a friend's house while they were out of town, and we could all go over there. I told them I probably shouldn't.

What? Did I really just say that? I said no to partying with three amazingly beautiful women? Someone smack me.

"Please go. We all go," Marla said.

"Okay," I said after getting my senses back. I guess I had more wine than I thought.

The house was literally two blocks away on the golf course. It was about eight thousand square feet of a house. We all walked into the kitchen, and Marla poured some drinks.

"There is a pool," Tina shouted from the family room. Less than a minute later, there was a splash.

I went out to make sure she was okay, and I saw her swimming. And her blue dress was on a lounge chair. Steph was right behind me and was getting naked. And, splash.

"You get in too?" Marla asked.

"No. You get in if you want," I told her.

Her dress was off in seconds.

The women played like little girls in the water. They were made-up Barbie dolls just a few minutes ago, but now their makeup was washed off, their hair was wet, and they were having fun. They were still beautiful.

Oh, yeah, and they were naked—or close to it. It was a fun evening, but I didn't stay.

I saw Marla a few times before she left town. It was interesting talking with her—learning about her childhood, growing up in Russia, and how she came to the US. She was different from American women. She was sexy, confident, womanly, and passionate, with no agenda and no drama—just enjoying the moment, which is kind of refreshing.

But unlike Greg, I didn't get a Russian bride.

Next.

DRAGON

Chelsea worked in my company's district office, and she came to my office about every six to eight weeks. She was tall and pretty, with long medium brown hair. She was about ten years younger than me, and she seemed nice. She was also single.

I really didn't know Chelsea well. All of our conversations had been pretty much work-related. She was in good shape, and she told me that she was training for a triathlon. In a work environment, it's often hard to get to know someone personally.

One time she was in the office, she was staying overnight to go to another office in the area the next day rather than driving two hours home and then back the next day. So she invited the office out for drinks.

About ten to twelve showed up, and there was the usual socializing. Everyone left after a drink or two, and it was just me and her left.

We ordered a couple of appetizers and sat in the corner of the bar and talked. I noticed one extra button was undone on her shirt, showing a bit of breast that I hadn't seen before. We talked about work and a little about our personal lives.

She was kind of flirting and was awkward about it. One time, when she moved, something in her shirt caught my eye. I think it was a tattoo. A minute later, I noticed it again.

"Do you have a tattoo on your chest?" I asked.

"Yes," And she pulled closed her shirt a little.

I asked her about it, and after a moment, she pulled her shirt over to show me part of it that was above her bra. It was kind of dark in the bar, so I asked her what it was a tattoo of.

She said it was a dragon, and she showed me kind of how it went with her hand on the outside of her shirt.

"Why a dragon?" I asked.

"I don't know. I was dating a guy who had several tattoos, and he talked me into it. It seemed like a good idea at the time."

"Is that the only one you have?"

"Yes. It kind of hurt getting it around my nipple."

"I bet. What kind of dragon is it?"

"It's like a Chinese dragon. Want to see it?"

"Okay."

Right there in the bar, she unbuttoned a couple more buttons, slid her bra strap down off her shoulder, and quickly pulled her left breast out so only I could see it.

Yep, it was a Chinese dragon all right. It was like the tail started just below her shoulder and came down circling the bottom of her nipple.

"Cool," I said.

And she put it away.

She flirted a little more, but I wasn't going there. I wouldn't let it. She worked in the district office and had influence on a lot of things that went on in the office I managed. She approved things for us and had the ear of my boss. Nothing good could come from dipping your pen in company ink.

I never told anyone about her tattoo. I didn't want anyone in the office to think differently of her or me.

It's not every day you meet a girl with a dragon tattoo.

The next day, I asked Jenny and Mandy if they had a tattoo.

Jenny said in a very sarcastic tone, "Yeah, I have a picture of you on my ass!" Mandy went ballistic laughing.

Hey, I was just asking.

Next.

WINE DOWN
WEDNESDAY

I received a message one day from Cheryl. She was attractive and had a sweet smile. She told me she worked downtown and asked if I ever went to Wine Down Wednesday.

I had been a couple of times. It wasn't my favorite place, and the wine wasn't really good, but I agreed to meet her there. (I'm really not a wine snob; I just know what I like.)

I met Cheryl there after work, and we sat at an outside table.

"What do you do?" I asked.

"I'm a secretary."

"Where?"

"Smith & Co., CPAs."

"Have you traveled much?"

"Not really."

"What do you do for fun?"

"A lot of things. Nothing special."

She wasn't much of a conversationalist. It was like pulling teeth to get her to talk. I couldn't tell if she was shy, lacked confidence, or nervous. Or maybe that was just how she was.

I was trying to coax her into getting involved, but she couldn't. I was using my interviewing skills, asking open-ended questions to give her a chance to talk, but she didn't. It was awkward for me, almost painful. I wanted to get the check, but I couldn't.

I told a couple of stories and got her laughing, but still not talking. She seemed to be enjoying herself, but she was not a social butterfly. I felt kind of sorry for her. I need more interaction.

All of a sudden, she started smiling and looking embarrassed. I was sitting with my back to the restaurant, and I could tell she was looking at something behind me, so I turned to see.

In the window were two women smiling, waving, and giving her the thumbs up. Then, they saw that I had turned and saw them. Their eyes got big, and they tried to disappear. Cheryl was about mortified. They were carrying on, making a spectacle of themselves, at Cheryl's expense.

I felt like I was in high school.

"Friends of yours?" I asked.

"Yes," she said.

She just sat there, red faced. And she never really said much more after that, except "Bye."

As she left, I saw Mandy and a couple of her friends, and she asked me to join them. Thank goodness—real conversation.

Next.

MONKEY SEX

Chris and I had both had one of those days. We were about the only ones still in the office when we were leaving and decided to go out for a drink. It was just a short walk to a nearby restaurant that had a good bar.

Chris and I were talking about our day—stresses in the market, hassles with clients, and girls. We both always dressed in professional business attire—good suits, sharp ties, shined shoes—and paid attention to details. And some of the women in the bar noticed.

One pair of girls sitting at a nearby table tried to start a conversation with us. They weren't particularly attractive. I mean, it was 6:30 p.m., not like it was "last call." Besides, Chris and I were talking business, enjoying the wine, and I was really getting into the bacon-wrapped shrimp and scallops we ordered. The truffle parmesan popcorn was pretty tasty too.

We saw a couple of groups of attractive women come into the restaurant and go into a private dining room. Then, a group of three came in, and Chris knew one of them. They waived to each other, and the three came into the bar. They were all very pretty and were wearing sexy dresses.

Chris introduced me to his friend, Tammy, who in turn introduced me and Chris to her friends. One was a CPA, and the other was a doctor at a local hospital. Both were in their early to mid-thirties—about ten to fifteen years younger than me. Chris and Tammy were catching up, and I was trying to entertain the other two.

Our conversation lasted about two minutes before they said they were all going to a girlfriend's going-away dinner party there at the restaurant in the private dining room.

After they left, Chris talked about how he knew Tammy—that she was an attorney and that they had dated a few times and remained friends. He didn't know her friends. I told him they seemed nice, and we agreed all three were hot.

After a second glass of wine, we each headed home.

The next day in the office, around 11:00 a.m., I received a text: "How about some monkey sex after work. Lori."

What? Who's Lori? And what is monkey sex?

I immediately went to Chris's office. He was on the phone, but I went in anyway and handed him my phone. "I'll call you back," he told whoever he was talking to as his face broke into a huge smile.

"What the heck!" I said.

"That's funny," Chris laughed.

"It must be a wrong number."

"No, Tammy said her friend Lori wanted your number, so I gave it to her. Lori was the doctor last night. Good job!"

"You gotta be kidding me. First, she's too young, and second, I don't even know what monkey sex is!"

"I don't either, but I'm willing to learn!"

It was about to digress into more of a frat boy dialog, so I went back to my office.

Am I that much out of touch? I didn't have any idea what monkey sex was, so I Goggled it. I didn't find much more than a bunch of YouTube videos, and I didn't like Dave Chappelle's description. Was there a trapeze bar above her bed?

Chris came in. "Did you reply?"

"No, and I'm not going to."

"Why not?"

"No."

Chris was disappointed, like his giving my number out was his attempt at matchmaking, but it didn't work. He was closer to their age. He was "very active." I wasn't. It was more up his alley, not mine.

I wondered, while she was very attractive, how often did she have monkey sex? How many others had she sent them to? Was that how she set up meetings with guys? Was she just horny, or did she have such low self-esteem that she felt she needed to do that to attract men?

Clearly, there was a lot I needed to learn, and some things I just didn't need to know.

Jenny laughed and told me to stay away from younger women—well away. Again, she was probably right.

Next.

I'M A JERK

I recognized Audrey's online picture from some business meetings, but I had never met her. We had a few short phone conversations, and I learned she had never been married, had no kids, and had just been made a partner at her law firm. We agreed to meet for lunch downtown.

It was a nice day, so we decided on a table outside. We started talking, and she was a total professional, like I was someone she worked with or a client.

"What's the matter?" I asked her.

"What do you mean?"

"When we talked on the phone, you seemed more relaxed, more natural. Now you seem like you're on a business meeting."

"Sorry. I didn't realize."

And we continued to talk. The conversation was better after that—for a while.

"So how do you handle complaints that clients may have against you?" she asked.

"I don't know. I've never had one. How about you?" I replied.

"No, I mean in general."

"I guess they ask questions to try to find out what happened."

"Who decides on settlements? Does the threat of an arbitration or lawsuit increase the settlements?"

I felt like I was on trial.

"Am I being cross-examined, or being pumped for information?" I asked.

Her eyes got big, and she looked at me like I had three heads.

"No, I was just trying to learn more about your business."

"There's more to my business than lawsuits. I help people."

"Yeah, I'm sure you do. But don't you ever feel like you have conflicts of interest between you and the products you offer?" she continued.

"Not at all. Why would you ask that?"

I was now remembering why people generally don't like lawyers.

"Just wondering how you handle the ethical issues in your business."

"I don't have ethical issues. What are you trying to get at?

"Don't you have ethical issues? It's all over the press, talking about increasing regulations. How would that affect you?"

"I would do whatever is required. I always put the interest of my clients first."

"Is that hard to do?"

"Is it hard for you?" I asked.

"I don't have ethical issues," she said.

"Is that why there are so many lawyer jokes?"

I could tell she didn't find any humor in that. Again, she was looking at my three heads.

"Well, if the interrogation is over, I need to get back to my office," I told her. I was only half finished with my lunch. I was irritated.

"Why? Did I insult you?" she asked.

I handed my credit card to our server.

"I'm not insulted, just disappointed. I thought we were on a date."

"We were."

"Do you grill all of your dates?"

"I wasn't grilling you! I was just trying to learn more about you."

"It didn't seem like it."

"Seems like someone has thin skin or has something to hide."

Okay, I was about mad now.

"I'm not even going to acknowledge that comment," I said as I signed the check.

"Guess I hit a nerve."

"You can't help it—you're a lawyer. Good luck." And I walked out.

"Jerk," I heard her say.

I hate dating.

I didn't try to be rude. I always try to be a gentleman, but she didn't appreciate it. And I know some women don't, and some never will. Some don't because of the women's liberation thing, some because they want to feel or act independent, some because they don't know how to be treated like a woman by a gentleman, some just don't have a clue or were never taught manners, and some have ulterior motives.

Some women act as if being a gentleman is a bad thing. Well, I'm not changing. Somewhere, there's a woman who will appreciate me as I am.

She was forty years old and had never been married, and I understood why. I guess there's someone out there for her, but I knew it wasn't me.

I talked about what had happened with Jenny. She just shook her head.

"Some women make the rest of us look bad. You know what you call fifty lawyers on the bottom of the ocean?" she asked.

"What?"

"A good start!"

The nice thing about this date was that I was one date closer to my last first date.

Next!

CHURCH LADY NUMBER 2

Cheri sent me a message through Match, saying she knew she lived outside of my preferred range, but she was transferring to a job in my town and moving in the next sixty days. She wanted to meet someone in the area. She lived about two hours away.

She and I talked numerous times and talked about a lot of things. She never had kids but liked talking about mine. We had a lot in common. She liked that I went to church. I told her I went, but I was no saint. She asked a lot about my church since she would be looking for a new one here.

Our schedules each had the next Saturday free, and she invited me over to go out and then go with her to church the next day.

When I got there, she was really pretty and kind of petite. Her blonde hair was in a cute style, almost shoulder length. And her townhouse was very nice—roomy and well-decorated. She showed me where my room was and let me freshen up after my drive.

Cheri poured us a glass of wine, and we sat and talked. She had a friendly long-haired cat that checked me out. She told me I was the only guy she invited to stay since her divorce four years ago.

We ate at a sushi restaurant. The food was good, and so was the company. After talking so many times, we knew a lot about each other and felt comfortable together even if it was our first date.

I showed her pictures of my kids—I love smartphones. She showed me pictures of her nieces. We talked about her new job and moving. She was pretty excited about it.

And she asked me about my church—the music, the programs, etc.

After dinner, we went to a famous wine bar. I think there were over a hundred wines by the glass on their menu. In the bar, she was getting more romantic, sitting close and kissing me. We shared a dessert. As soon as we were done, we went back to her place.

On the drive back, Cheri was holding my hand and said, "I really want you to stay in your room tonight, no matter what."

"Okay."

We sat on her couch and made out for a while. Cheri said she was tired and needed to go to bed. We went upstairs and got ready for bed. She came into my room to make sure I was comfortable. She sat on my bed, and she kissed me good night. We started making out again.

"I have to go to bed," she said as she stood up. "Good night."

"Why don't you stay here?" I asked.

"I want to. I really want to. I *love* sex. But I don't always make good decisions. Stay in here. Promise?"

"Promise."

Cheri walked out of my room into hers. She left both of our bedroom doors open. As I went to sleep, I thought about her trying to be a good girl, and we were going to church together in the morning.

Several hours later, I was woken up by Cheri as she got into bed with me. She got under the covers and snuggled up with her back to me. I held her. She moved her hips back and forth into me, and I told her to stop and go to sleep.

I wanted to help her be a good girl. I really try to be a gentleman, but sometimes I don't always make good decisions either.

I woke up in the morning and she was still cuddled up against me. I just lay there. I felt her wake up, and she started with the hips again. I got up and went to shower before anything got started.

I didn't want to do anything that she might regret or anything that would make her feel bad about herself. I love sex too, but there's a time for everything. If there was going to be a relationship, there's no need to rush things. It's not always easy trying to be a gentleman.

We went to church. The service was good and the music was great. Afterward, we went out to lunch. Then I headed home.

The office she worked in offered her a promotion to entice her not to move, and Cheri took it. We talked a few more times, but I never saw her again. I was glad for her, but it was a shame—she had potential.

Thought I might get the chemistry right, not the timing. Again.

Sometimes life just gets in the way of your plans—hers and mine.

Next.

IRISH PUB

Maureen and I communicated a few times. She said she traveled quite a bit for her job, so trying to meet was difficult. She was flying back into town on a Friday afternoon, and we tentatively agreed to meet after work if she was up to it.

Around 5:00 p.m., she sent me a text that we should meet at an Irish Pub/Restaurant close to where she lived on the north side of town. I was familiar with the place. They often had a decent band. It was about forty-five minutes from my office, so I started fighting rush hour traffic. As I left the highway, I texted her about where to meet, and she said to meet at the hostess stand by the bar.

I finally get there, and there was almost no parking. There are several restaurants and bars close to each other in the area with shopping and a movie theater, and they all seemed full. I texted her that I was walking to the pub now, but there was no response.

The restaurant was very crowded and loud when I walked in. There were a lot people inside and outside waiting for a table, and the bar looked pretty full too. I looked around when I got into the pub, but I didn't see her. I walked around the waiting area, then the bar, and still I didn't see her. I waited a few minutes in case she was in the ladies' room. Still nothing after a few minutes.

I walked into the bar again. There was a group of guys in a heated dart game, a very boisterous group, a couple making out, a group of women having a bachelorette party, a lot of people having a good time, and it was loud—normal bar scene, but no Maureen.

I went outside looking at the patio tables, still no sight of Maureen. I texted her again. Nothing.

Across the street was a quieter wine bar, more my style. I ordered a glass of cab, sat down, and waited for her to reply. When I was finishing the last sip and thinking it was time for me to go home, she replied. She said she had been sitting on a bench just inside the bar. I told her I'd be right over. I couldn't believe I missed her. Did she not look like her picture? Wasn't she looking for me too?

And there she was, sitting on the bench where I saw the couple making out. Wait a second! She was half of the couple that was making out!

She stood up and said hello.

I asked her, "Weren't you just making out with a guy here?"

"Yeah, but it's nothing."

"It didn't seem like nothing."

"No, really, it was innocent."

I was thinking, playing tonsil hockey while a guy is getting to second base in a bar was a little more than innocent!

"Do you always have a pregame warm-up before a date?" I asked. She looked surprised, like I had offended her.

"Come on, don't be an ass," she said.

Was I missing something? Was I being an ass? Was there a hidden camera and I was getting punked? Okay, deep breath. Be calm.

"Let's get a beer. There's a couple of barstools opening up," she said as she motioned toward the bar.

Against my better judgment, we sat down and ordered a couple of beers. I paid for the beers and, before I had the first sip, told her I needed to use the restroom. I was back in less than five minutes, but she was gone—and so were the beers!

I knew I should have left earlier. For some reason, Jerry Springer came to mind. I imagined she was going home to her double wide.

I walked back to my car, trying to get a handle on what had just happened. I couldn't believe it. Do real people act like that? Half mad, half chuckling, I just shook my head. What else could I do? As I was driving out, I saw Maureen and her make-out buddy sitting at an outdoor table, drinking my beers!

Cheers.

(Note to self: leave when your gut tells you to.)

Monday, back in the office: "Jenny, you're not going to believe this."

"You find some winners," she replied afterward.

Next.

BABY NEEDS A DADDY

I met Connie at a café for dinner one night, and she told me her life story. She was a pretty platinum blonde in her mid to late thirties. She had been a pharmaceutical sales rep, and since her divorce, she was now going to college to become a physician's assistant. Her ex-husband lived out of state, and she had a two-year-old son, Andrew.

We talked about a lot of things. She was interesting. Then, the conversation took a turn when we talked about our kids.

"You sound like a great dad," she said.

"Thanks. You're obviously a good mom."

"I try, but it's hard. I'm so busy with school. And Andrew needs a daddy."

I just about choked.

"Kids are amazing. They can adapt to about anything," I told her.

"I want Andrew to have a daddy. A boy needs a dad," she said. "I bet you were great with your son. You seem to have a lot to offer."

I was getting nervous. I think I actually started sweating. Connie was nice, but I didn't know she had a young son when we first talked. I'm sure the boy was nice, but my youngest was sixteen. I really didn't want to raise another baby. That's really a young man's game. I didn't want to be drawing Social Security when he was graduating from high school.

My kids were older. Most of the tough work was done—you teach them right from wrong, and you hope something sticks.

I was looking forward to starting to enjoy my life as my kids were becoming independent. I would enjoy my time with them, but I would have time to travel and do things I wanted to do, not what they wanted to do. I liked the thought of grandkids one day, but I also liked the thought of giving them back.

I know that at my age, most people have families and any future relationship is a package deal—all or nothing.

I never saw Connie again.

Mandy came by and asked me about my date.

"She was nice, but she had a baby. It's not the situation I'm looking for. Too much work," I said.

"Then you shouldn't date women in their thirties," Mandy replied. "Either they have babies, or they want babies. And the closer they get to forty, the louder their biological clock is ticking. Even if they say they don't want kids, they all want kids."

I know she was right. I guess my target was the post-biological clock woman. Problem is they don't wear name tags.

Next.

CATHY'S FRIEND'S FRIEND

I met Cece at a party a year or so earlier. I remember her as a tall, very attractive woman. Someone told me she was a Miss Florida runner-up about twenty-five years earlier, and I could see that. She was definitely a Barbie doll type. She was also described as a party girl who never really grew up.

I saw her profile on Match, and I sent her a message. She replied, and we met for Sunday brunch. When I called the restaurant to make reservations, they told me that Sunday was their monthly disco brunch. There are a lot of gays that live in that area of town, and I heard some of them kind of got into the theme. I told Cece I had no problem with it, and she thought it would be fun.

When I knocked on her door to pick her up, two pit bulls came to the clear glass door, barking with their ears back. I didn't want any part of them. Cece came to the door and closed the doors behind her.

"They just bark a lot. They're harmless," she said. "They're really sweet dogs. Pit bulls are so misunderstood."

Sure. I always associated pit bulls with harmless and sweet. I guess that's why they are on TV for attacking and mauling small animals and children.

Cece looked fantastic. She was about five feet nine, slender, in a cute short dress with a low-cut front, showing a lot of cleavage.

We talked like we already knew each other. She was very bubbly, and she could talk about anything. In some ways, she seemed like a twenty-five-year-old in a forty-five-year-old body—a very hot body.

The song YMCA was playing when we walked into the restaurant, and there was a crowd dancing to it in the bar. I think I saw a drag queen—not exactly what I was expecting.

We sat and talked about her business and our common friends. We were having a great, fun conversation. Cece did a lot of volunteer work too. She had a big, good heart.

She told me I had met one of her best friends on a Match date, Madelyn. I told her I only took her out once, but she already knew. I didn't tell her how her friend came on to me. I told her I also knew Madelyn's friend Cathy. I didn't tell her I dated her though.

It was hard not to look at her chest. I was pretty sure her cleavage was man-made. Either way, they looked nice. I also noticed her eyebrows didn't seem to be moving much.

About that time, a guy came over to our table and hugged Cece. It was her hairdresser. He introduced us to his "friend."

Cece had never been married, and she said her dogs were like her kids. She had a lot of girlfriends—married and divorced. I think she went out almost every night, either with friends or dates. It was like she wanted a relationship, or even a husband, but she didn't want to give up any of her social life for the relationship. It almost seemed like a social immaturity or immaturity on relationships.

Lunch was leisurely and relaxed. After lunch, we did some window shopping before I took her home.

When we got to her house, Cece invited me in. I heard the dogs barking before we got out of the car. Cece went in first, moving the dogs away from the door. One was older, and the other was about a one-year-old puppy. The puppy was excited, and she held him by the collar, trying to calm him down.

I was petting the older one, and the puppy seemed to be settling down. Cece was talking to him. When she let go of him, he was off like a shot and headed toward me.

I was pretty calm while this sixty-pound pit bull jumped into my chest with his mouth open. He jumped hard and knocked me back. The next time he jumped, he bit my shirt and tore it.

"No! No! Down!" Cece said like a not-too-serious mom scolding little kids.

The dog jumped a few more times, leaving slobber on my shirt and pants. It was acting like an uncontrolled child. He wasn't viciously trying to attack me—more like being excited. He never did actually bite me, but my shirt was history.

Cece started chasing the dog with a spray bottle. The other dog was barking, and it was funny watching her chase the puppy in her short dress and very high heels, trying to squirt him while yelling in a sweet, half serious tone "No!" and "Down!" Dog running around, her jiggling and chasing him, and water being sprayed all over the place—a comical scene.

She finally got him by the collar and put him in the garage. All of a sudden, I had a thought from the book *Marley and Me* and what kind of damage the dog could do out there.

She was very apologetic and embarrassed, saying the pup never misbehaved like that. I had my doubts. I tried tucking my shredded shirt back in and said goodbye.

Cece was nice, there were some things I really liked about her, and she has a lot to offer. She was fun. Not that we had a future, but when you date people at my age, you don't just date the woman; you have to look at the whole package: kids, pets, history, everything.

And the "baggage" can sometimes be the deal breaker.

Jenny asked how my date was.

"Great. A Barbie's dog ate my shirt."

"What? Oh, this ought to be good," she replied.

Last January, she posted on Facebook that her New Year's resolution was to have a husband by year end. I saw her recently post that she had a guy and was going to meet his parents at Thanksgiving. I wonder if she took her "kids."

Next.

WINE PARTY

A few of my friends and I had gotten together after work, and we were talking about all kinds of things—work, kids, spouses, exes, and the topic turned to what kind of wine some of us were drinking.

I told them I was thinking about selling my lake house, and they all said I needed to have a party there before I sold it. I suggested a wine party, and they all thought it would be a good idea. I asked if any of them would help me, and I didn't get a lot of support, but they all said they would come.

So it was on. I started to think about a theme and what I wanted to do. I talked with Adam, a friend of mine who is a wine supplier, for some ideas. I told him I wanted to make sure I had wines for people who liked reds or whites.

We thought about having a variety and decided to have a theme of Wines of the World. Adam said he and his wife would come and help pour the wines.

I expected thirty to thirty-five people to come, so I started to choose wines and buy them. I figured for a tasting, I could probably get five to six glasses per bottle, with a glass of each wine for thirty-five people, plus some extra.

I bought seven bottles each of a Napa chardonnay, an Italian super Tuscan, and a Chilean Cabernet, and nine bottles of French champagne. That was thirty bottles for just over $800. This was good wine, not Yellow Tail.

I thought about food for the party and decided to cook everything myself. I had a fruit and cheese platter with the champagne as everyone arrived, then seared scallops in a truffle beurre blanc sauce with the chardonnay, cheese tortellini in marinara with the super Tuscan, and a beef tenderloin with a gorgonzola sauce and chocolate with the Cabernet.

I bought plates, napkins, and forks. I rented wine and champagne glasses and some tables and chairs for the deck; I really had everything set. I didn't realize how expensive and how much work parties could be.

I invited a few friends, some coworkers, and close neighbors; about forty invited and thirty-two coming. I was happy with that. Jenny, her husband, and her sister, Chris and a date, and Mandy were all there. It was a good mix of guys and girls, couples and singles.

I put together a party playlist that was playing, and people started to arrive about thirty minutes before sunset. We all went lakeside to watch it. It was about 74 degrees that night with low humidity—perfect!

The champagne was fabulous. The other wines were opened when the food was ready and served. Wine flowed, people talked and laughed, food was eaten, and everyone was having a good time. I received a lot of compliments on the food and the wine. I was kind of busy cooking, but it was fine. My friends were having fun.

There were a few single girls there; one brought a girlfriend. One of the girls thought she was my date for the party, but she wasn't. She kind of acted like it, though, and followed me around.

It's funny how the higher the wine consumption, the higher the flirtation factor becomes. And a couple of the guys and some of the women were definitely turning it up.

A few people were sitting at my bistro table talking, and I was leaning on one of the chair backs. One of the girls came up and stood to the side of me, with her breast in the back of my arm. I didn't react. A minute later, her hand was rubbing my back, and it was soon on my butt.

We went out to the dock for a few minutes and kissed a little. The moonlight was reflected in her big brown eyes. I soon realized she was drunk. About that time, my "date" came out and sat on the dock. We were all talking. Then my "date" looked at me and gave me the hair flip and a smile. About that time, another couple came on the dock, and we went back to the house. My "date" didn't like me helping the drunk girl back.

It seemed like there was always a couple or a group on the dock. They should be out there on such a great night.

Uh-oh! Someone said we were out of wine! I had a wine cooler with about two hundred really good bottles, and another four hundred bottles in closets, so I started to pull bottles from the bedrooms before they got into the good stuff!

A little while later, another woman asked me, half slurring, if I wanted her to stay to help me clean up. I thanked her but told her I had it under control.

My "date" said she couldn't drive home, and asked to stay. I told her I had a couple of extra bedrooms if she wanted even though I don't think that's what she had in mind.

Around 1:00 a.m., the last of them went home, and I did a little cleaning of stuff that would spoil or be really gross by morning. I thought it was a great party.

The next morning, I was cleaning up and counted forty-eight empty wine bottles. Whoa! That's forty-eight bottles for thirty-two people. No wonder everyone had such a good time!

There were glasses, plates, and napkins all over the place. I saw some trash on the dock and went out there. Picking up a couple of plates, I saw a bra. Well, I didn't notice it there when I was out there last night. Someone had a really good time!

I'm not exactly sure whose it was. I thought about who was there and may wear a 34-C. I know bras are expensive. Maybe I should send an e-mail to everyone asking who might have left it. I went back to the house.

Then I heard something in my extra bathroom. It was my "date," and she looked rough! I didn't realize she actually stayed.

"Do you have coffee?" she asked me.

"I can make you some. Do you need some Tylenol or anything else?"

"Yes, please. Have a toothbrush?"

"Sure. By the way, are you missing a bra?"

In the office on Monday, Jenny said, "Great party! Hubby and I had a great time!"

"Good. Hey, do you—" and I stopped myself. I could tell she probably didn't wear a 34-C. Definitely.

Next.

HELD UP

Chris often came into my office on Monday mornings to tell me about his weekend conquests and experiences. He walked in and sat down. He didn't have the normal smile and energy he usually had.

"You're not going to believe what happened," he said.

"What?"

"I met a girl Saturday night who I met on Match."

He paused.

"Okay," I said.

"We met at a club downtown. You know—drinks, dancing, hanging out. Things were going well, so she followed me back to my place."

Another Chris story. Now for the gory details I really didn't want to hear.

"And she robbed me."

"What! Are you kidding me?"

"Really. Just about five seconds after my door closed, she pulled a gun out of her purse. She took my wallet and my watch."

"I can't believe it!" I said.

"I can't either."

"Which watch were you wearing?" I asked.

"My Tag watch. And there was a couple of hundred dollars in the wallet, plus credit cards."

"Then what? Call the police?"

"Yeah, they came. They kind of laughed. Her cell was evidently a disposable one and untraceable. I didn't get her license tag. And her Match profile is down, so there's no picture. She didn't have a very good picture posted anyway. She contacted me first. The cops didn't think there was much chance of getting her."

"That's unbelievable."

"Yeah. But hey, I got the female cop's number."

"Of course you did."

Next for him too.

TWO TOPS DOWN

Margo was someone I had done some business with related to my business for a couple of years. She was always friendly and outgoing and always had a smile. She was about fifteen years younger than me.

We talked over time and became friends. One night, I was out with Chris then I saw her, and I finally asked her out.

We had a great time, going out several times. She had a great personality and was really a lot of fun. Margo was always smiling and laughing. She drank beer, liked football, knew wine, and sometimes wore a baseball cap. Yep, she could have been a dude. But for a tomboy, she could dress up and looked good doing it too.

Margo introduced me to some of her eclectic friends when we were out downtown. Some kind of reminded me of the group of friends from Napoleon Dynamite. One slept with everyone, another stole boyfriends, and one was a total geek. She had guy friends too, and she was definitely more comfortable hanging out as one of the guys—until they started teasing her. She could give it out, but she couldn't take it.

One night when we were going out, I picked her up, and she was frustrated with her roommate about something. I had never met the roommate before, but Margo had told me about her. She was evidently a bit of a slut and a slob. Then I saw her—numerous tattoos, several piercings, and dressed like, well, a slut. Margo said she had had a few glasses of wine while she got ready and had to deal with her roommate.

We were going to dinner before a basketball game. Dinner was fun. We ate, drank, and laughed.

The game was good close to the end, with a lot of athletic plays. And there were more drinks to go to keep the feeling going.

The parking garage was packed as the crowds left, and traffic was backed up. We couldn't even back out of our space. We were on a high floor, so we weren't going anywhere for a while. So we made out to kill time.

Somehow her shirt was unbuttoned. When her bra came undone, things fell out of her bra.

"What the heck are those?" I asked her, half laughing.

"Those are my chicken cutlets."

"Huh?"

"Padding."

I just kind of laughed while I looked at her and her breasts, and she smiled with those breasts she had showing from her open shirt. They were kind of cute.

I knew she had small breasts, and I just found out they were smaller than I thought. I think my man-boobs were bigger than her breasts.

We were finally able to move. It was a beautiful night, and I put the top down on my convertible. A few minutes later, we were on the highway.

She kept trying to distract me. Then she just took her shirt off. I looked at her, and she smiled and giggled. We were driving down the highway with the top down on the car and her shirt and bra on the floorboard. She really was fun.

I thought of her more as a friend, thinking we were keeping things pretty loose rather than thinking romantically. Later, I realized she might have been thinking more on the romance side, though. I guess it was bad timing, or probably more like bad communication, and that would be my fault. She kind of understood me; she got me when few ever have.

We're still friends today, and I'm glad.

Next.

ARE YOU PULLING MY LEG?

Debbie came up on Match.com as someone with similar interests as me, and I was someone whom she may have an interest in. She was a professional, and she was really cute! Her profile said she was five feet ten and was about ten years younger than me. I like tall blondes, but what guy doesn't?

We talked numerous times and texted back and forth. She was from South Africa and spoke with an accent that was quite soft. I liked listening to her talk. She was busy, often traveling with her work. It was a busy time for me at work too, and my kids had things going on, so we had a hard time scheduling time to get together.

Finally, we set up a meeting and met at a casual restaurant after work one day. When she walked in, she was very pretty! She saw me, came over, and kissed me on the cheek.

"I like tall guys, so I can wear heals," she said.

She ordered a South African wine and I teased her, asking if she worked for the South African Chamber of Commerce, and she replied, "I could do the job better, but they couldn't afford me." A quick, sharp wit is something I like, especially from a cute tall blonde with an accent.

She had done extensive traveling, with her job being travel industry—related and in visiting family in Europe and South Africa. We talked about where we had each traveled and about our businesses; the conversation was going well. It was interesting to listen to her tell about living and growing up in South Africa. She was very sweet.

We ordered another glass of wine and kept talking.

A few minutes later, I think the second glass of wine started to hit her.

"You have really nice lips." she said out of the blue. "I bet you're a good kisser."

"Well, thank you. I haven't had any complaints."

"Do you like kissing?" she asked.

"I do if I'm kissing someone who kisses me the way I like to be kissed."

"Oh! Well said! I like that. I like kissing—a lot."

I wondered if she did kiss like I liked.

"You know what really gets me going?" she continued.

"What?"

"I really like my nipples pulled. It's the key to everything else. It, like, opens Pandora's box." Sounds like it opened Debbie's box. One glass and a few sips of wine, and she was drunk.

And she wasn't done.

"Kiss them, suck them, and pull them. The more you touch them, the better I like it."

With that, the couple in the next booth was looking at us. Oh crap!

I never knew South African wine was such an aphrodisiac! Maybe I'm just that much of a hunk? No. Sorry, ego, the signs were clear—she was drunk. In addition to not having much of a tolerance for alcohol, she also evidently had a small bladder and had to go to the ladies' room for the second time since she got there.

As she got up, the couple next to us was still looking at me. The guy had a wry smile on his face. I noticed some people I knew in the restaurant. I really didn't want to be embarrassed, so I tried not to look over there.

As she came back to the table and sat down, she took a big gulp of wine. I told her it was getting late, and I probably ought to get going.

She said she lived just a few blocks from the restaurant and asked if I would walk her home. Being a gentleman, or at least trying to be a gentleman, I told her I would. I didn't want anything to happen to her on the way home. She finished off her glass.

When we got outside, I asked her if she knew the way home, and she said she did. The whole way there, she was all over the place talking about her job, about how good the wine was, and of course, about her nipples. A couple of times, she grabbed her breast while she was holding my arm.

For some reason, the song "Tequila Makes Her Clothes Fall Off" was playing in my head.

We walked less than ten minutes and reached her place. She fumbled with her keys. Finally opening the door, she invited me in. I told her I didn't think that was a good idea and I should go home. She started to pout like a little girl—sad puppy eyes and bottom lip out! Trying to back out smoothly, I told her I was very flattered, she was very attractive, and maybe another time.

She then stepped out of her doorway down to the step I was on outside and kissed me—hard. Her tongue was not going to be stopped by my lips. Her shirt was unbuttoned slightly, and she moved my hand onto her breast so fast I hardly knew what happened, and held it there. Did she wrestle hippos in Africa? She was strong and determined!

I left her safe in her house. On my way back to my car, I couldn't help chucking a little. I was not on safari to bag one that night.

The next day, I tell Jenny what happened.

"Are you pulling my leg?" she asked.

Well, something wanted to be pulled.

(I later googled to see if South African wines had aphrodisiac affects—no more than any other wine. I'm sure it was me, then.)

Next.

CHANGED HER MIND

In my online profile, I said I would not respond to anyone who didn't have a picture in their profile. I mean, if my picture is there and they can see me, isn't it fair I see them too?

Tabitha sent me a message online, asking me to please give her a chance. She said she would send some pictures to my regular e-mail address. I read her profile, and we seemed to have a lot of common interests. Okay, what did I have to lose?

I sent her my e-mail address, and the next morning, there were some pictures. She was beautiful, so we talked and texted back and forth a few times.

She flirted about the theme on my profile—about timing and chemistry being hard to get right.

On one particular call, she started flirting a lot.

"What are you looking for in a woman?" she asked.

"A woman who is attractive, smart, fun, and affectionate." I told her.

"I'm all of that and more."

"Really? How?"

"If you play your cards right, you might find out. Are you a good kisser?" she asked.

"I think so."

"We'll see about that."

And we agreed to meet for lunch a few days later.

It was a beautiful day, and the restaurant where we met was on a lake with an outdoor patio, and that's where we got a table. She showed up in a cute sundress, and she was even better-looking in person. She had a great smile, and when she smiled, it was like her eyes lit up.

The conversation was good—we had differences of opinions, but we had fun talking about them. It was playful and flirtatious. She reached for my hand a couple of times. I had to get back to work, and she held my hand while we kissed goodbye. She said she liked the way I kissed. There seemed to be some chemistry.

Tabitha liked live music, so a couple of nights later, we went out to listen to a local band. The lead singer was a friend of mine. When I picked her up, she looked fabulous in her tight jeans and high heels.

It was a fun night—dancing, singing, talking, and laughing. I introduced her to my friend in the band. Later, we went back to her place, and I stayed a little while.

The next morning, I woke up and went to work out. As I was coming home from the gym, I got a text from Tabitha.

"Thanks for a great evening, I had a great time. I really like you, but I have some unresolved feelings for my ex and I want to give it another try. Good luck."

What!

I believe an ex is an ex for a reason. I also know better than arguing or trying to change a woman's mind.

"I thought we had chemistry. Just bad timing, I guess. Good luck to you too," I replied.

I was a bit disappointed in this one. Another one whom I thought had potential.

I talked with Jenny about it, trying to see if I did something wrong. She didn't think I did.

It's true. Chemistry and timing are hard to get right at the same time. It's also true there are other women out there. Lots of women, so . . .

Next.

BROWNIES AND
MARGARITAS

One day, I was searching through profiles when a new one came up as someone who shared a lot of common interests with me. Missy was very pretty in her pictures—five feet ten, slender, long blonde hair, and blue eyes—definitely my type. Not long after I sent her a message, she responded.

Not long after, we met for lunch at a sushi place close to my office. Missy looked like a forty-year-old Barbie with bangs. She dressed smartly, with all kinds of David Yurman jewelry.

We immediately hit it off. She was a model since college. I remembered some of the TV commercials she did when she told me about them. We were having a great time. In addition to being beautiful, she was very sweet and nice too.

We talked about all kinds of things—our kids, her pothead brother, her no-good ex-husband. I like lunch dates because I always have the excuse that I have to get back to the office and they rarely lasted more than an hour. This one lasted over two. In fact, she invited me to go to a party with her the next night before she kissed me goodbye.

I picked her up that evening, and it seemed like we picked up right where we left off earlier.

The party was fun. It was at the house of a friend of hers. It was a twelve-thousand-square-foot house (the owner told me). There were over a hundred people there. I knew a couple of people, others looked familiar. It was a fun crowd. A band played by the pool.

They were serving wines I had only heard about—way out of my budget—and they had cases of them. Missy liked them too. She told the female host of the party how much we liked the wine, and she set aside a few bottles for us to take home. These were $200 bottles of wine! Anyway, we enjoyed the whole thing—location, wine, food, music, people, and the company.

It was getting close to 10:00 p.m., and we decided to leave as Missy lived about thirty minutes away and she had a babysitter with her daughter.

"Those desserts really looked good," she said. "I should have had one."

"I tried not to look at them, but they seemed to call my name. Do you want to stop and get dessert?"

"Where would we go?"

I pulled into Chili's.

"Trust me," I told her.

While she was in the ladies' room, I ordered two El Presidente margaritas and a brownie a la mode. When they were brought to our table, she smiled.

"I love margaritas and brownies, but together?" she asked.

"Just go with it. There are no food police in Chili's."

We both had a great night. We closed Chili's down, and I took her home. I hope her babysitter wasn't mad.

We would see each other several more times until I realized there was a problem—she had an alcohol issue. I also learned that she had a history of using men to get what she could and then she would find another. A good friend of mine from high school who had modeled with her and had known her for years filled me in on her history.

And the baggage and bitterness she had over some of her exes were more than I wanted to deal with. I didn't need a gold digger, and I definitely didn't need an alcoholic who was bitter. At times, I saw flashes of Cruela De Ville in her. It's a shame that someone so beautiful outside was very ugly inside. It surfaced randomly, more so when she drank. And she was mean to her daughter too.

Last I heard, some guy had just bought her a new Lexus. Good for her, I guess.

Funny, the more you get to know someone, the more you notice the warts. Maybe the key is to find someone with warts you like.

I still have a couple of bottles of that wine and better memories of the wine from the party than I do of her.

Next.

BUTT PRINT

Denise was about five feet nine and was a bigger girl than I typically saw. She wasn't fat—just big-boned, curvy, toned, and well-endowed. She was pretty, with a great smile and a great laugh. She was like a forty-five-year-old brunette version of Anna Nicole Smith. She had a cute small dog too.

We went out a couple of times, and she was affectionate and not shy. Maybe sexy and confident is a good way to describe her. She would stand next to me with her breast against my arm, put my hand on her leg, and wear very low-cut dresses—definitely provocative.

It was our third date, and I picked her up at her apartment. She had some wine open, so we had a glass and talked. She was being very affectionate.

She and I walked to a Thai restaurant a few blocks away for dinner. We had a great time talking, drinking, and flirting. Denise was in the travel business, and she talked about her adventures. We finished a bottle of wine with dinner and were feeling pretty good.

"I caught you looking at my breasts," she said smiling.

"It's hard not to notice. They look like they could fall out of your dress pretty easily."

"They could," and she pulled one out of her dress right there at the table.

"Wow!" I said as she rubbed her finger over her nipple.

She smiled and put it away. Luckily, the restaurant wasn't crowded, and I don't think anyone saw her. Like I said, she wasn't shy.

What kind of woman does that in a restaurant? That has never happened to me before. Do women really do that now? Was I that much out of touch? I didn't know the answers to those, but I did know her doing it turned me on!

We were walking back from dinner with my arm on her shoulder and her arms around me—she was rubbing my chest with one hand and grabbing my butt with the other.

On the way back to her place, we saw some of her friends sitting at outside tables at a bar. They asked us to join them.

Denise introduced me and said we'd stay just a little while. They had been there a couple of hours drinking before we got there. They teased me about going out with her and joked about her too. The conversation was fun.

After a glass or two, it was getting late, so we left them.

We both had serious buzzes going on. In her building elevator, we were kind of all over each other.

When we got to her place, we both had to go to the bathroom. She went first. When it was my turn, she got the leash to take out the dog for his turn, and we all headed to the elevator to walk him.

As we walked to a park about a block away, we were still being affectionate to each other. We found a place in the park on the back edge away from the road that was pretty dark, and she sat on a utility box in the shadows.

We were kissing and touching. She pulled up her dress while she sat—she had no panties on (did I mention that she wasn't shy?).

I looked around—there were people walking through the park. We were in public, but no one seemed to notice us. It was like I could see them, but they didn't see me. I was excited but nervous. After a few minutes, the dog was ready to go. So we went back to her place.

The next day around noon, she texted me.

"I'm at brunch with some girlfriends, and I told them about the park last night."

"Oh, really?"

"They are sooo jealous! Jeannie from last night thinks you're really handsome!"

"Tell her thanks."

"I was walking the dog and tried to find which box we were on. Do you remember which one it was?"

"Look for the one with your butt print on it."

An hour later . . . "Found it!"

Next.

DON'T HATE ME

"Hi," I said as I introduced myself to Tonya.

"Hi. I'm ready for a drink," she replied.

"I'll have one of what he's having," she said to the bartender.

"Rough day?"

"Aren't they all? Especially when you work for a total dickhead."

Well, okay then. I guess she didn't have a good day at work. When I had talked with her on the phone, she seemed nice.

"It seems like something might have set you off. What happened?" I asked.

"It's always something with that douchebag. He complains about every little thing I do. It's like he's watching over my shoulder just trying to find something to bitch at me about. And I'm tired of it!"

"I can tell."

"He never complains about the other girl in my office. You know why? Because he's doing her! Everyone knows it. I wouldn't play his game, so now he rides my ass, trying to get me to quit so he can replace me with someone else to put in his harem."

"Really? Have you thought about going to Human Resources?"

"We *are* Human Resources!"

"Oh! I can see how you'd have a problem."

"Men are all the same!" she stated.

Okay, this was starting to get good. How can I have fun and still not get myself into too much trouble?

"How's that?"

"They all just want the same thing."

"To be loved?" I asked.

"Yeah, right," she said as she was starting to get a bit red faced. "Men don't know what love is except for their cars and their food. They think love is sex. You know why a man's penis has a hole in it? To get oxygen to his brain."

"Really? So why do you date men?"

Okay, she was now looking at me like I just landed from outer space.

"You don't seem to have a high opinion of men. Why are we on a date?"

"You know, most men have their heads up their asses."

"I'm not most men."

"You're divorced—you're damaged. If you were so great, you'd still be married."

"If you were so great, you'd be married too."

Ooops! Shouldn't have said that! Now I was in trouble. She was totally red faced, with fire coming from her snout, salivating, and daggers shooting from her eyes. Dragon Lady had arrived in all her glory.

"Let me tell you something! I have a lot to offer! And men are just posers and users, thinking they can take whatever they want and do whatever they want whenever they want! And you're just like all the rest of them! You're all assholes."

"Ouch! Does someone need a hug?" I can't believe I just said that.

Mission Control, we have liftoff!

"Don't you touch me! See! You're just like every other guy! Grab me! Cop a feel! Is that your game! You disgust me!" And she went on like that for another minute or two.

Mission Control, we're about to go into second stage booster ignition.

"Were you abused as a child, or have you always been a man-hater?"

She was looking at me with that alien look again. But at least she was quiet—for a moment.

"Why would you say something like that? There are lots of women who have been abused! And it's insensitive guys like you who make it worse! And I'm not a man-hater!" She ranted and raved for a couple of minutes.

I interrupted her. "Why are you here? To get a free drink?"

Again, a pause. But now her eyes were starting to tear up.

Mission Control, we may be about to either enter into orbit or come crashing back to earth.

"What do you mean?" she asked.

"Why are you on a dating website? Why do you date? Why did you agree to meet me here tonight?"

"I want to find a good guy."

"So you can verbally abuse him? And do you think he'll like being talked to that way and being treated that way? Because you've been a bitch since you walked in. How many good guys want some of that? You said you have a lot to offer. All you've shown me is attitude. It's not attractive at all."

Pause. "You're right, I'm sorry. I had a bad day," she said as a tear finally rolled down her cheek. Crash.

The old saying is right: you don't get a second chance to make a first impression, and this was a first impression I couldn't get over. She was yelling at me within two minutes of walking into the restaurant— and it was our first meeting. And she called *me* damaged.

Okay, she had a bad day. We all have bad days once in a while, but that doesn't give anyone the right to take it out on anyone else. I admit I shouldn't have stirred the pot, and I could have been more understanding and sympathetic. If she's like that on a first date, how bad might it be if she really knew me?

The next morning, Jenny asked me about my date.

"Guess why my penis has a hole in it," I told her.

"I don't want to know any details about your penis, especially if you got it pierced."

"No, I didn't!"

"Good. Then stop talking about it."

Next!

FLY AMERICAN

Diana and I had some great conversations on the phone. The problem was our schedules. I work normal business hours, and she was a flight attendant with a hectic schedule. Plus, she lived on the opposite side of town, about a forty-five-minute drive, which made it difficult for us to meet.

Finally, she was in town one weekend, so we met for lunch on Saturday. We met at a restaurant, and she greeted me with a hug and a kiss on the cheek. Diana was a kind of curvy brunette with steel blue eyes. She was about five feet five, and it looked like she worked out. She was wearing a cute summer dress that flattered her figure.

The conversation was very natural. She had been a flight attendant for twenty years and had traveled the world. She talked about how she used to sightsee on her layovers while working, but now she didn't as much. She said she had been some places so many times, she got bored with them. She said as she got older, she didn't like working overseas flights as much anymore.

Still, we talked about our travels. She really had been to a lot of places and seen a lot of sights. She was nice and interesting to talk with.

"Are you one of those people who can talk to anyone and make them like you?" she asked.

"I can usually talk with most people," I told her.

"You have a very cool, calming way about you."

Thank you, I think to myself.

Lunch went well.

"My best friend is having some people over this afternoon, and I was going to drop by after our lunch. Would you like to go with me?" she asked. "I mean, if you don't have other plans."

"The only plan I had today was to meet you. Sure, I'd like to go."

She smiled.

I followed her to her friend's house. It was a huge house on a lake in a fairly exclusive neighborhood. It was easily a two-million-dollar house. Her friends needed to open an account with me!

Her friend and her husband were nice. There were about twenty people there. I ran into a guy I had met a few times. We sat outside by the pool. There were a couple of TVs on with college football on.

They had hired a guy who played his guitar and sang, providing some entertainment. When he took a break, one of the host's daughters came out with a guitar and played and sang for us. She was really pretty good.

I was mixing and mingling with the people there, and Diana was usually next to me. All the people there were nice, and I'd like to get some new contacts for possible accounts—at least get to know my acquaintance a little better.

"You really can talk with anyone. You don't know anyone here, but you fit right in," she said.

"It's a gift."

We were there a couple of hours; some of the games were ending, and some of the guests were starting to leave. I figured it was time for me to leave too. Diana was going to stay a while longer. I said my goodbyes to everyone, and Diana walked with me outside. She told me she had a great time and kissed me goodbye.

"I hope I get to see you again," she said.

"I'm sure you will."

"I leave in the morning for a flight, but I will be back Wednesday."

"Okay."

On Monday afternoon, I texted her: "I hope you're having a good flight."

About an hour later, she texted back: "It's work. Took you long enough."

"What do you mean? I know you were working."

"I expected you to call sooner."

"Sorry. I didn't know I did anything wrong."

"Well, you did."

"We can talk about it when you get back."

"Don't worry about it. We're done."

"Really?"

"Really. Good luck."

Wow! She said I could talk with anyone, but I didn't know what to say right then. I was surprised and disappointed. I saw her Saturday, she left town to work on Sunday, and I texted her Monday—and I waited too long?

How was I supposed to know what her expectations were? Did I do something wrong, or was she unreasonable? I don't know. Was she insecure and needy? Better to find out about any issues earlier rather than later.

I asked Jenny and Mandy to help me understand. They just shook their heads.

Next.

BUTT DIAL?

Dina was a thirty-eight-year-old divorced mom who had recently moved into the area for her job. She worked full time, had eleven—and seven-year-old kids, and got up at 5:30 a.m. every day to work out. She said she did one hundred crunches a day.

I liked talking with her. We had a lot in common: we're both in financial jobs, had MBAs from big schools, worked too much, are active with our kids, and tried to stay fit. We talked and texted several times.

It was hard to meet because of her kids' schedule with sports, and she was on a limited budget, so child care in the evening wasn't easy. She really didn't know a lot of people here.

I offered to arrange and pay for a babysitter, but she said she'd take care of it. She finally arranged for a sitter, and we went out.

It was nice to meet her after talking with her as many times as we did. She was cute in her sleeveless dress. I could tell she worked out—her arms, shoulders, and calves were ripped.

We went to a nice Italian restaurant for dinner, and she seemed glad to be out. No kids, no boss, no demands—a relaxing dinner. She mentioned it was nice having dinner with adult conversation.

Dina missed her parents and sisters when she moved here with her job. She had been divorced for two years. She seemed lonely.

Dinner lasted three hours. It was a good conversation, and there seemed to be some chemistry. We made plans to get together the next week.

I took her home. We had some great kisses. Then I said good night and went home.

I had a really nice evening, and it seemed she did too.

A little while later, I was getting into bed and I got a text. It was from Dina.

She texted: "Good night, babe. Hope you had a good day."

I texted back: "I don't think you sent this to the right guy. I'm not 'babe.'"

I never heard from her again. I had an unsettled feeling about it.

"Mandy, have you ever sent a personal text to the wrong person?"

"Yes."

"What did you send? How did it turn out?"

"No comment."

Next.

BLACK TIE

Annie and I had been acquaintances for a couple of years. She was very active with several charities, and she told me she was busy planning different events for some of them.

One day, she called me in the office.

"Hey. What are you doing next Saturday night?" she asked.

"Nothing much," I responded. "Why?"

"I have an event that night, and I wanted to see if you would go with me."

"Okay, I'll go."

"Great! Do you have a black tie?"

"Of course, I do."

"Good."

We talked a couple of times before the date. The entertainment for the event sounded good, and I was looking forward to going.

The event was being held at a big hotel, and Annie had to be at the event several hours before it started, so she told me to meet her there.

I took my time getting dressed. I like wearing my tux. It was kind of fun getting all dressed up sometimes. I thought I looked decent in a tux.

I texted her that I had arrived, and I headed toward the ballrooms.

As I was walking to the ballroom, I saw conventioneers and some people that were dressed in western attire.

Uh-oh. As I approached the registration desk outside the ballroom, I noticed the western-dressed people were going into my ballroom. And the women at the registration desk were dressed in western clothes too. Big uh-oh. I was starting to have a bad feeling about this. This had the potential to be embarrassing.

I went to the desk and asked what event this was for. Yep, I was in the right place—forty-five minutes away from home and the event was starting in twenty. I texted Annie to meet me at the registration desk.

Annie came out wearing a cute denim skirt with a matching vest, cowgirl hat, and boots. She looked adorable and started laughing when she saw me.

"James Bond meets the Wild West!" she said. "Patent leather shoes are almost like cowboy boots."

The registration ladies were looking at me, chuckling, realizing I was her date. Okay, I was now officially embarrassed.

"I thought you said it was black tie!" I said.

"When did I say that?"

"When you asked me to the event, you said it was black tie."

She started laughing again.

"Oh, yeah! No, I asked you if you had a black tie. I wanted to borrow it for an outfit I needed."

She kept laughing. I did too. There's no reason to get mad—just make the most of it.

"I thought I sent you an e-mail with the event announcement and details," she said. "I'm really sorry. You look great though."

"Thanks. You look great too."

"Let's go in. I have some friends I want you to meet."

We went into the ballroom. A lot of people looked at me. Annie wasn't embarrassed to be with me even though I felt totally out of place not being dressed for the occasion.

The music and entertainment were good, and the people at our table were fun. It was a good evening, and there were plenty of jokes about me being confused with the wait staff.

Annie and I never did date other than that event, and it really wasn't a date. It was a nice evening, she was nice and we had fun, but there was no chemistry at all—for either of us. That's okay.

But hey! I won a round of golf for four as a door prize!

Next.

It's a Gusher

I arranged to meet Anne for the first time at a sushi restaurant on a Friday night. It was a popular restaurant with good food, and they had a large outdoor patio with comfortable furniture. She texted me that she was having a drink with friends on the patio and that I look for her out there.

When I arrived, I walked out there and ran into a girl I know from college, Liz. I hadn't seen her since college, and she looked the same. She was there with about eight others for a birthday. I talked with her just long enough to say hi.

I saw another group of women, and Anne was sitting there with them. They were all looking at me. I walked over to them.

Anne stood up and smiled as I got close. She was about five feet nine and slender. She was blonde with a cute hairstyle and was wearing a long light blue linen dress. We met on Match.com. She was sitting with four friends.

We hugged hello, and she introduced me to her friends. They were all checking me out.

Wait a second! The first woman looked familiar. Think quick, think quick! I know—I saw her picture on Match.

Wait another second! I recognized another from Match, and I'm pretty sure we sent messages to each other, but then I wasn't interested.

Another looked kind of familiar. I wasn't having a good feeling about this. Awkward!

I just stood there and pretty much smiled while Anne got her purse and said goodbye to her friends. Then we headed inside the restaurant, and I waived to Liz.

"Who was that?" Anne asked.

"An old friend I hadn't seen since college. She was a little sister for my fraternity, and she dated one of my frat brothers. She was always nice."

"Pretty too."

As we sat down, Anne said, "Some of my friends knew you from Match."

Now it was really getting awkward!

"A couple of them looked familiar to me."

"The brunette on the end said she had talked with you."

"I never talked to her, but I remember exchanging messages with her once."

"She's such a slut. She met a guy and had sex with him in his car the first night they met."

What do you say to that? I just smiled and shook my head.

"All of us in the group are on Match, except for the other brunette who's married. We all saw you online, and we all talked about you. They're jealous because I got to date you first."

It was like I had to meet them all so she could brag and show me off as her prize.

"Do you plan on passing me around?"

"No, but some guys have dated a few of us, and they didn't know we knew each other."

"That's kind of weird," I said.

"I guess I'm the prude. I won't go out with someone they've had sex with. Did you date any of them?"

"No."

"Good. They said they hadn't dated you, but I don't always trust them."

This was still very awkward.

"What if they don't tell you who they've had sex with?" I asked.

"Are you kidding me? They couldn't keep a secret if their life depended on it. They can't wait to tell us who they were with. And they include all the details."

Yep, still awkward.

We ordered and talked about other things. Anne was a teacher and seemed very caring in the way she talked about her students and her children.

I'm kind of a touchy guy—I talk and put my hand on someone's arm, or sometimes I put my hand on a woman's shoulder when I'm sitting by them.

And when I did this with Anne the first time, she flinched.

"Oh, I'm sorry. I don't mean to be forward," I said.

"No, it's fine. I'm just a little sensitive. I like it, really," she replied.

Every time I touched her, she flinched. I tried to be more conscious about it, trying not to touch her.

"You're a good conversationalist," she said.

"Thank you. It takes two to have a conversation. Otherwise, it's a sermon."

She laughed. We talked for a while longer.

After a few drinks, she was sitting a little closer, and I had my hand on her leg, or shoulder, or arm. Anne kept flinching.

It was getting late, so we decided to call it a night. As we got up, Anne was feeling the back of her dress.

"Everything okay?" I asked.

She nodded her head yes.

As we got outside, there was better lighting, and I saw something on the back of her dress.

"There is something on the back of your dress. Did you sit on something?"

"No," she replied as she started to blush. "I have a bit of a problem."

"Sorry, I didn't mean to embarrass you by saying anything." I was just trying to help.

I knew she had been to the bathroom a couple of times. I guess she had a bladder control problem. Don't they make pads for that? Dang, I'm getting old! I'm dating women who need diapers!

"It's okay," she said. "I told you I was sensitive."

What? It's my fault she has this big wet spot on the back of her dress?

"What do you mean?" I asked.

"I'm so embarrassed. I'm easily stimulated. This is really humiliating."

Oooh! She is overly self-lubricated! All kinds of thoughts were going through my head. Talk about leaving a wet spot! It was kind of intriguing and, at the same time, kind of gross. Okay, couldn't she use a panty liner? Especially if she knew she has this condition?

I could tell she was embarrassed. I tried to joke that guys can't always hide their enthusiasm and ours is right out in the front. She smiled.

I didn't dare kiss her for fear of her creating a puddle, plus I was worried about her getting dehydrated.

I've been to SeaWorld and watched Shamu, and I didn't want to be in the splash zone.

And I definitely wasn't going to tell Jenny.

Why do I seen to find the "different" women? I was getting kind of discouraged in my search. I tried to stay positive, knowing that each date with the wrong woman was getting me closer to finding the right woman. I know she's out there! I hope she's looking as hard for me as I am for her.

Next.

LUNCH HOUR

Jodi was a forty-two-year-old brunette. Her pictures showed her as tall and slender, and her profile said she had never been married and had no kids.

Generally, I won't meet someone who has never been married. I prefer someone who's been married because they tend to be more flexible, they understand compromise, they're usually less self-centered, and, even if it failed, they have experience in a longer-term relationship and commitment.

I've learned there's usually a reason they've never been married. They often say they just never met the right guy.

Occasionally, they had been in a longer-term relationship and never married, but more often they had been busy with their career, busy having fun (party girl), couldn't really keep a relationship going, or some other issue.

Oh, yeah—or they're just wacko.

Jodi worked close to my office, and after e-mailing a couple of times and talking once, we agreed to meet for lunch.

We agreed to meet at a pizza place a couple of blocks from my office. I was right on time, and as

I walked up, Jodi was already there waiting for me outside.

We greeted each other with a hug, and I asked if she wanted to get a table inside or out.

She looked at me and said, "I only have an hour for lunch," while she pointed at her watch. "My apartment is across the street."

She didn't want pizza for lunch—she wanted sausage!

I immediately wondered how often she did this. It wasn't anything I was interested in. I'm not into sluts. We had just met about twenty seconds ago!

I think I just found out why she had never been married.

"Listen, I'm really not into that," I said.

"Really? Are you kidding me?" she said.

"Really, and I'm not kidding you," I told her.

"Unbelievable!" she said in a huff.

You should have seen the look on her face: mad, frustrated, surprised. She was obviously pissed off that I turned her down. I guess that didn't happen to her often.

And she just walked off. Well, maybe she kind of stomped off.

She just made another case for not seeing someone who's never been married.

I went in and ordered a couple of slices to go with a cannoli for Jenny and Mandy.

Next.

You're What?

"What are you doing Tuesday night?" Chris asked as he walked into my office.

"I'm free. What's up?"

"I was talking about you with Debra last night."

"Wait, who's Debra?"

"The girl I've been seeing for a couple of weeks. Didn't I tell you about her? She has a friend she thinks would be perfect for you. Her name is Amanda."

"Wait a second, she doesn't know me."

"I told her all about you. Debra says she's hot."

"Where'd you meet Debra?"

"In the elevator."

"Of course."

Reluctantly, I agreed.

Even more reluctantly, I told Jenny. She gave me an earful.

"You shouldn't hang out with him. Do you want a reputation like his? Guilt by association! You ought to know better," she scolded me. "Isn't that what you tell your kids?"

Tuesday came, and I met them all at a tapas restaurant. Amanda was very pretty and about ten years younger than me. She was an attorney at a large law firm. It was a good evening, with fun conversation.

We all had to work the next day, so we decided to call it a night. I walked Amanda back to her car and kissed her good night. We both agreed to talk the next day to make plans to see each other again.

We ended up going to lunch later that week and dinner that weekend. Things were going pretty well. We talked and texted.

On Monday, she called me to go to lunch. I was free, so I met her.

She talked about some office politics and a new case she just started.

"Listen, I need to tell you something," she said.

"Okay."

"You're a really great guy, and I really like seeing you, but I'm engaged."

What? She's what?

"If you're engaged, why did you go out with me?"

"Well, I did it as a favor to Debra. I don't think she knows I'm engaged. When I met you, you were pretty cool. And I guess I was having doubts about the engagement. I kind of got caught up in it, and I shouldn't have done it. I shouldn't have used you, and I'm sorry. You'll be a great catch for some woman."

Am I the only guy this kind of stuff happens to? Sometimes I think there's a cloud hanging over me in the relationship department.

I told Chris what happened.

"Debra thought she might have had a boyfriend, but she agreed to see you. Whatever!" Chris said. "Did you tap it?"

What? Did I tap it? Maybe Jenny was right—I didn't need to hang out with Chris and his friends.

"How was your date with Chris's friend?" Jenny asked.

"She's not my type," I told her. Married and engaged women have never been my type.

Less than a year later, Amanda was married.

Next.

OUT OF TOWNER

One Saturday, I was on Match.com when I received an instant message.

"Hi! You sure are cute!" popped up on my screen.

"Hi," I replied. I tried to access her profile, but it was not posted.

"You have a great profile. I really like your pictures too."

"Thank you."

"Want to know about me?" she messaged.

"Sure." I guess she was into some kind of games. Okay, I'll play.

"Good. I'll unhide my profile for a couple of minutes."

I looked at her profile. She was pretty, had three kids, and had a good job.

"What do you think?" she asked.

"Why do you hide your profile?"

She said she didn't want her friends to know she was on an online dating site and didn't want to be recognized by her clients. Okay, I can buy that. She lived in a small town about forty-five minutes away.

We talked a few times, and we agreed to meet for dinner one day that I was meeting with clients in her area.

I was pleasantly surprised. She looked better in person—long, nearly black hair and steel-blue eyes. And she was wearing a cute strapless summer dress. She hugged me and kissed my cheek when we met.

She spoke with a soft southern accent and told me she was raised in the South. It was nice talking with her and listening to her. She had traveled the world as a flight attendant prior to her marriage, and she was very interesting. We talked mostly about travel and kids. We had a lot in common.

She asked me if I could give her a ride home because her son needed the car and had dropped her off. I told her that was a big risk on her behalf. She said she had a back-up plan with a girlfriend to get home if needed.

We walked around the docks and boardwalks surrounding the restaurant. We were both having a good time. I drove her home.

She liked red wines and suggested we go in and open a nice bottle. She pulled off the rack a great bottle: it was a 2003 Dunn Cabernet. I had never had it before. It was really smooth, and so was she. I had more than I should have, and she talked me into staying. I stayed in the guest room.

I got up early and drove home in time to get ready for work. Later that day, I called her to try to see her again. She told me she had a great time with me, but she was really kind of seeing someone.

What? Now I understood the secrecy. She had her profile hidden so her boyfriend wouldn't find out, and she would find guys online from outside her city. Seemed she had everything planned that evening too. Clever.

I thought there might have been potential. I don't find many who I wanted to date a second time, but once again, I was disappointed. At least the wine was not disappointing. It was actually a pleasant surprise. I bought a few bottles next time saw it in a wine shop.

(Note to self: You get in trouble the further you get from home—especially when you drink.)

Next.

I Don't Need That

Cyndi's profile picture showed her standing in front of a giant wine rack. That got my attention. Plus, she was hot—slender, long dark hair and blue eyes. Her profile had a lot of similar interests with me, and on her other pictures, it seemed like she had a bit of an adventurous side. And she knew a lot about wine.

After talking a few times, her sharp wit and sense of humor was evident. Cyndi seemed fun. We knew some common people, and I asked them about her. She probably did the same about me. She got good recommendations. Soon after, we decided to have dinner on a Saturday night.

She asked me to pick her up. When I arrived, she opened the door wearing a sexy dress, and she looked great in it. She had opened a bottle of 1998 Krug Champagne, a fabulous, expensive, bottle of bubbly. I love a good champagne, and this was a very special bottle.

"Wow! What's the occasion for such a nice bottle?" I asked.

"I won it in a silent auction and was anxious to open and try it."

"It's very nice of you to share it with me. Thank you."

"You're welcome. Have you ever been to Napa?" she asked.

"Not yet. I've been to wineries in Tuscany, Bordeaux, and Spain, but never Napa. It's on the top of my list, though."

"It's wonderful. The food, the wine, the culture. I can't wait to go back."

"This champagne is fantastic!" I told her. "I've never had it before."

"I'm glad you like it. I've never had it before either."

Then she showed me her wine cooler. She had quite a collection, with over four hundred bottles, mostly reds. We kept drinking and kept talking.

We later went to a bar that had some live music and pretty good tapas. It was like we already knew each other. The conversation and interaction was smooth and natural. The company, wine, food, and music were all great.

We danced, drank, and enjoyed the music and the company. We both seemed very comfortable with each other. It was a nice evening.

She was affectionate. She would lean into me with her hand on my leg—more so on the way back to her place. Cyndi invited me in for one more glass of wine.

She lit a few candles. I was pouring a couple of glasses of the leftover champagne when she came into her kitchen wearing a short robe that was partially open.

"You look great," I said.

"Thanks."

About that time, she slid a sample pack of one Viagra tablet to me.

"I don't need that."

"You will."

Wow! That's bold! And aggressive. She obviously knew what she liked, and she wanted everyone to be prepared. I wasn't sure how I felt about that.

Things kind of went downhill from there for me. She came out of her closet wearing a pair of Nike's.

"What are the tennis shoes for?"

"Traction. I kind of get into it. It's been a while."

She didn't kiss the way I like to kiss. And she did things, or tried to do things, I didn't really care for. She had a good time, but I felt like a NASCAR driver in a five-hundred-mile race, just clicking off laps trying to get to the finish line.

I wasn't saying a word about this one to Jenny. And I don't need Viagra.

Next.

I SEE DEAD PEOPLE

Lisa sent the first message. She told me she lived and worked fairly close by, which made things convenient. While I prefer tall blondes, she was very attractive, slim, with dark brown eyes and hair. She was fun to talk with. We hit it off pretty well the first time we talked.

We agreed to meet at a nicer restaurant close to her house. I was waiting in the bar for her to arrive. The lounge had live piano music that was actually pretty good. She arrived, and we ordered a good glass of wine. Just as the wine arrived, the power went off in the restaurant. A few minutes later, the manager told us the power company people were on their way, and it would be at least an hour before the power was back on. We decided to go elsewhere. We rode in my car and noticed all of the businesses in the area were without electricity. We decided to go a few exits up the interstate to another area of restaurants.

We saw an upscale steak house, and she said let's go there. She had a gift certificate for the restaurant that she never had a chance to use. So we did. Dinner conversation was as good as the steak and wine. She was very personable, flirtatious, smart, and with a good sense of humor—all traits I appreciate in a woman. Not to mention she was very attractive.

The conversation continued to flow. I asked her about a scar on her arm. She then told me she got it in a bad auto accident she had several years earlier.

"I actually died in the accident," she said.

"Really?"

"Yeah. I saw the light and was drawn to it. I wanted to stay."

"What was it like?"

"It was amazing—soothing, calming, peaceful, like aaahhh," she sighed. "I was supposed to cross over, but for some reason, I'm still here. I came back into my body."

"Wow."

She definitely had a more serious look. The date was now crossing into the *Twilight Zone.*

"It's a curse," she said.

"What do you mean?"

"At night, I'm visited by spirits whose bodies died but their souls haven't crossed over. They come to me as a fellow spirit, looking for guidance with what they should do. I have a body, but they don't. They are confused."

What? They couldn't have been any more confused than I was.

"I see dead people. They wake me up, wanting advice. Sometimes many of them will come to me during the night. I don't get much sleep some nights. I tell them to go back to the light. When I sleep with someone, they leave me alone, though." She paused. "Would you stay with me tonight so I can sleep?"

That was the most creative pick-up line I had ever heard. Creepy but creative. For some reason, Elvira came to mind.

I know there are a lot of things I don't understand and there are a lot of things in the world that cannot be explained. But I did know that I never liked horror stories, and this date was getting way too weird for me.

I drove her back to her car at the first restaurant and said good night. While spirits may visit her at night and keep her awake, I was not doing either. I wasn't willing to sleep with more than one person, and I had no idea how many more I'd have to share the bed with if I stayed with her.

Well, she seemed normal at first, and I guess she held it together as long as she could. I think she believed what she was saying. I wonder what her shrink thought. Sometimes I think there are hidden cameras on my dates just to see my reaction.

All the way home, I kept looking into my rearview mirror, expecting to see a ghost from Disney World's Haunted Mansion in the backseat. And I slept with the bathroom light on.

Next.

WHO'S GEORGE?

I met Adrianne in a store where she worked. She was gorgeous—light brown hair with highlights and big brown eyes.

We went out a few times and were getting to know each other. She was originally from the Midwest, with an eight-year-old son and a seventeen-year-old daughter. She worked hard in a retail job, got pregnant at a young age and never got any further education, and had a strained relationship with her ex-husband. Her daughter was a handful—rebellious. And Adrianne thought she may have been into drugs.

Adrianne did the best she could, but she was struggling. She said didn't date much, and was so appreciative to be eating out somewhere other than fast food. She was fun at times, but other times she was pretty negative—maybe from stress, maybe from her life experiences. I wasn't sure about all of this.

We had only been going out a few weeks, and she called me.

"Can I come over for a minute?" she asked.

"Sure. What's up?"

"I'll see you in a couple of minutes."

She had never been to my house before. When she arrived, I could tell she had been crying.

"What's the matter?" I asked.

"I'm in trouble, and I don't know how to get out of it," she said.

"What kind of trouble?"

"Financial."

"How much do you need?"

"Four hundred."

"Okay. I'll help."

"Really?" she said as she hugged me. More tears came down.

"Give me a minute."

She sat on my couch as I went in my bedroom to get her the money. I had a stash of cash in my dresser.

"Here's $500," I said as I gave it to her. "There's a little extra to help out."

"Thank you," she said as more tears came down from those big brown eyes. "I can't pay you back."

"That's okay," I said.

"I can work it off," she said.

"What? You want to work it off?"

"Yeah."

"Like what? Cleaning my house? Ironing my shirts?"

"I could, but that would take a long time. Let's go to your bedroom, and I'll work it off."

Wait a second. What? She wanted to work it off with sex? I started feeling sorry for her. I had no idea she was this desperate.

"No, I'm not going to pay for sex. I'm giving it to you—no strings attached."

"Really? You are a good man. Thank you so much."

And she left. There was a bill she had to pay before some place closed, probably a power bill. I didn't ask.

The next day, I told Jenny.

"You're too generous. You shouldn't do that," she said.

I was raised by a single mom who worked in retail, had a difficult ex-husband, and struggled financially. I understood what she was going through. I had to help.

A couple of days later, I called Adrianne.

"Hey! Let's go out and get Chinese food tomorrow night," I said.

"Listen. I know this probably looks bad, but George moved in with me."

"Who's George?"

"He's kind of my boyfriend."

What? Are you kidding me? She goes out with me, asks me for money, offers to have sex with me, and she has a boyfriend? I felt pretty stupid. Was I that gullible? Was "sucker" written on my forehead? Was this her plan? I felt set up and used. Okay, Jerry Springer, where's your film crew? I thought I was doing the right thing.

I gave her the money, and I got screwed.

All Jenny said was "Told you so."

I hate when women say that to me, even if they are right.

I told Chris.

"You idiot! You should have done her!" he said.

"No, it wasn't right." I said.

"It would have been more right than you think!" he replied. "Besides, if it floats, flies, or fornicates, you're better off renting it anyway."

"Chris, I want more than that. Don't you want to be held and loved?" I asked.

"Sure. Then I want her to go home! Maybe she could make me a sandwich before she leaves."

I laughed. Then I said, "That's the difference between you and me. I want to find someone who wants to stay."

I could make my own sandwich. I could cook and clean by myself. I could do my own laundry and ironing. I didn't need someone to do that for me. I wanted someone who wanted to spend time with me—because of me.

Lesson learned.

Next.

TENNIS LADY

I met Judy on Match about a year earlier. She was really nice. While our chemistry wasn't good to be a couple, we did become friends. Judy was an avid tennis player.

One day, I got a text from her that she has a friend she thought would be great for me. I really don't like blind dates or fix-ups, but Judy said to trust her. So she sent me Becky's phone number.

I called her, and she seemed nice, so we arranged to meet for a drink one night.

It was a nice evening. I lived a mile from the restaurant and decided to walk. I took an umbrella because it looked like it may rain.

I got there about ten minutes early and texted her that I had a booth for us in the bar. She replied she was running ten minutes late. About the time she was getting there, a really bad thunderstorm started. It was like a monsoon outside.

She texted me that she got there, but she didn't want to park and get out of her car because of the lightning. I texted her back, saying to pull up to the front door and I would come out and get her and park her car.

It was pouring, wind was blowing, and lightning was flashing all over the place. It was nasty. Becky pulled up to the front door, and I went out with my umbrella. She got out, and I walked her inside, trying to keep her dry. Then I went back out into the elements and parked her SUV.

When I got back into the restaurant, I was pretty much soaked.

"Thank you for being such a gentleman," she said. "I appreciate gentlemen, and you went above and beyond. I almost just went home when I got here. Then you offered to come rescue me. How could I say no?"

"Thank you. I try."

Becky was also a tennis player. She had a cute figure and good tan, as you'd expect.

We talked, and I learned she had daughters that were the same as my daughters' ages, and they went to the same high school. She was also a college football fan, and our conversation was good.

About that time, one of my daughter's friends came into the restaurant and saw me with Becky.

A few minutes later, my phone vibrated; I got a text. I wasn't going to be rude and start texting. When Becky went to the ladies' room, I read it. It was from my older daughter.

"Who are you with?" she asked.

I'll respond later.

It was getting late, and I walked her to her car. It was still raining lightly, so she walked close to me under my umbrella.

"Where did you park?" she asked.

"I walked here. I just live down the street."

"Let me drive you home. It's raining."

When she parked in my driveway, I leaned over to give her a hug good night. But she wanted a kiss—a big kiss. She practically moved over into my seat. Her hands were all over me. She was trying to undo my pants and was ready to dive in. She moved my hand onto her breast. I was being attacked.

Whoa! I stopped her.

"Don't you like me?" she asked. "Am I not attractive?"

"No, that's not it. You are very attractive. I just don't like to go this fast. I need to go inside now. Good night."

She was obviously disappointed; it was all over her face.

"I met three guys this week, and you're the only one who stopped me," she said.

"Good night."

I guess I am a gentleman; shame she wasn't a lady. Three different guys in a week? Two didn't stop her? That's not the kind of woman I was looking for.

A little while later, my phone vibrated again. It was a text from Judy.

Her: "How was the date?"

Me: "It was nice meeting her. She's kind of aggressive."

"She likes talking about sex."

"She likes to do more than talk about it! LOL!"

"Seeing her again?"

"I don't think so."

"Sorry."

Then I got another text from my daughter: "Well?"

Me: "Do you know Brittany and Melissa from the next neighborhood?"

"Yes, they ride my school bus. Why?"

"I went out with their mom."

"That's weird."

"I won't see her again."

"Why?"

"Just not interested."

"Okay."

What I really wanted to say was her friend's mom was a slut, but you can't do that. At least you're not supposed to.

Next.

SMOTHERED

In Carla's pictures, she was beautiful. In talking with her on the phone, she sounded very nice. She was a mother of a thirteen-year-old boy, and she worked as a CPA for a private company.

We went out a several times, and we were getting along well. She shared custody of her son with her ex, and she had him every other week. We saw each other when he was with his dad. She was a very devoted mother.

I tried to see her a couple of times a week. I'd invite her to meet for lunch during a week that she had her son. The weeks she didn't, we would go to dinner on the weekend and maybe meet for a glass of wine after work. We got to where we would text once or twice a day and talk every couple days.

Carla was analytical, and her personality was a bit stiff, with no great people skills—maybe a little on the obsessive-compulsive side. Accounting was a good profession for her. Her house was meticulous. Even the refrigerator was immaculate and amazingly organized. At restaurants, she rearranged the table—where the salt and pepper were, how her silverware was placed, and so on. I moved a book on her coffee table, and she straightened it when she walked by later. She was very sweet as I got to know her, though. Oh, yeah, and she was hot.

We had been dating a couple of months when at dinner one night she says, "We need to make some changes."

"What do you mean?" I asked.

"We see each other once or twice a week. You're inviting me to do things all the time. I really like you, but it's smothering me. It's like you're trying to control me, and it makes you seem needy."

Needy? Controlling? Smothering? Me? I didn't get it at all.

"I like you, and I want to spend time with you. I didn't know I was smothering. I've never demanded anything, just invited. You've said yes to some things and no to others. I was cool with all of that."

"I know. The invitations are smothering me. They put so much pressure on me. And your texts. Maybe I need to tell you when I want to see you. Then we can make plans."

"What about my texts?"

"A couple of times you texted 'When can I see you again?'"

I never thought asking a woman "When can I see you again?" was offensive. I had no idea where she was coming from.

"Do you need more time to see other guys?" I asked.

"No, I'm not seeing anyone else," Carla said.

"So you like me, and you're not seeing anyone else, but you don't want to see me so much and I shouldn't try to see you as much?"

"Exactly."

"Okay."

Was I really putting pressure on her? I was just trying to date her. I liked her, and I wanted to spend time with her. I never thought seeing her once or twice a week was smothering. And she felt smothered just from invitations. I never tried to take her away from her time with her son. I really questioned her motivation and stability.

The next day at work, I texted her, "I had a meeting for Friday canceled. Are you free for lunch?"

"Didn't you hear a thing I said last night?" she replied.

"What? It's just an invitation. Say no if you don't want to go. I don't know why it's a big deal," I said.

"No."

She could have said she was busy, or came up with any excuse. Instead she just said "No." I took that as "No, I don't want to see you." I thought Carla's people skills and communication skills were not fully developed.

A little bit later, I called her to let her know just how needy I was. I told her I was sorry but this was not working for me, and I wished her luck in her search for someone special. We talked for a few minutes, and I could tell she was trying to hold back tears.

I want to have a relationship with someone who likes my company and wants to spend time with me, even if we only have time for just lunch. If they can't, a "Sorry, I can't, but can I get a rain check?" or "Would love to, but have plans. How about the next day?" or even "Can't, but I look forward to seeing you again soon," would be nice. Is that too much to ask? Maybe my expectations are too high.

It's amazing that a guy will often put up with a lot of stuff for a hot woman. Some guys put up with a lot for a long time. Not me. Life is too short to settle or be miserable. Relationships should be easy and natural, not stressful. I wondered what the real underlying issue was with her. I now wondered why she and her husband split. I hope she finds a counselor to help her.

Once again, a pretty outside doesn't always mean a nice inside.

"Hey, Jenny! Have I told you how nice you are? I appreciate you. You're pretty inside and out."

"Thank you! Now, what do you want?" she said.

So much for trying to be nice.

Next.

Ruth's Chris

I received a notice that Marlena was interested in me. Her profile was interesting. She was very attractive, very well-dressed, and classy. And in all of her pictures, she was in unique places. It also said she was a widow.

Her profile mentioned she liked fine dining, wine, the beach, and the arts. So I responded and sent her a message. We communicated a few times, and I called her after I got her phone number.

"You mentioned that you've traveled a lot. Where did you go last?" I asked her.

"Oh, I have been very fortunate to have met some great people who have taken me to a lot of wonderful places. My last trip was to St. Barts." She replied.

"I hear St. Barts is really nice—but expensive."

"It was very nice, but I really don't know what the trip cost."

"Wealth definitely has its benefits."

"Oh, I'm not wealthy. When I travel with a man, he takes care of everything. I'm a great travel companion."

What does that mean? I was looking at her profile while we talked. I noticed that she didn't say she liked to travel—she said she liked to be taken to nice places. I get it. He takes care of the expenses, she takes care of him. It's almost like she's a "travel escort."

"How long have you been widowed?" I asked.

"About twelve years. He left me in a position where I didn't have to work if I watch my budget. The market hasn't helped much lately, though," she said.

I'm getting the picture: she doesn't have to work, but to travel, she hooks up with a guy and probably suggests they take a trip. Does that make her a bit of a gold digger?

"How long of a relationship have you had since you became a widow?"

"Well, I've met a lot of really great men, but I really haven't seen any of them for more than about six months. I'm still looking for Mr. Right."

Okay, so she sees them, gets a trip or two out of them, the guy realizes he's being used and dumps her, and she's on to the next guy.

Wait a second. Was I just in a bad mood? Was I jaded? I didn't know her, but here I was making judgments about her. Come on, give her a chance. Don't be cynical.

"I saw that you like wine," she said. "What kinds?"

"I like big cabs and cab blends, and champagnes. What about you?" I replied.

"I like those too. I really like Quintessa, Peter Michael, and Cardinale. And with champagne, Cristal and Krug are my favorites," she said.

"I like those too."

I liked them; I just couldn't afford them. The Quintessa and Peter Michael were about $150 a bottle and the champagnes were over $200. She *should* like them!

"Maybe we should meet next week," she said.

"Sure, let's try to meet for coffee," I told her.

"I only meet for dinner, and I prefer Ruth's Chris for first meetings."

"That's a great restaurant. Why Ruth's Chris?"

"I believe a man should take me to my favorite restaurant. If he's not willing to take me there, we probably aren't for each other," she stated.

Yep, a gold digger. Or maybe just spoiled.

And I was being judgmental.

Well, I didn't need to spend $250 on dinner to know we weren't for each other, so I told her maybe we could talk again another time. That was the nice way of saying I'm really not interested. She probably thought

I was just cheap. And that's probably how she weeds out guys to find what she was looking for.

A few months later, I was at a business dinner with a group of about fifteen at Ruth's Chris in one of their private dining rooms. I came out to use the men's room, and someone caught my eye. I knew it was her. She was sitting at a table with a guy.

Sucker.

Next.

St. Lucie Set Up

My good friend, Ann, was in my office one day, and we decided to get a drink after work. She was my age, fun, interesting, a former college football cheerleader, and hot. Oh, yeah, and married. We were talking about my social life. She really wanted dirt on the women I was seeing and what I was doing with them. Ann wanted all the details.

"What kind of woman are you looking for?" she asked.

"One just like you."

She just smiled.

"I know a lot of eligible women. Want me to set you up?"

"Are some around here?"

"Not really. But I know some really attractive, successful women," and she pulled out her phone. "I know I have pictures of some."

"Naked?" I joked.

"No! You'll have to get those yourself!"

"You have any of yours naked on there? If not, I could take some."

Again, she just smiled.

Showing me a picture on her phone, she said, "Dori lives in Tampa. Doesn't she look a lot like me?"

"She doesn't hold a candle to you, but I guess I'd do her—for you. You know, take one for the team."

"Yeah, I bet. Here's Linda, she lives close to me. She's a lawyer."

"That's over two hours away! She's pretty, though. Tell me about her."

"Well, she's been divorced about five years and has two kids in their early teens. We see a lot of each other. She's fun."

"Come on, Ann, what does she look like? Who is she?"

"She's pretty."

"No. How tall? How much does she weigh? Fake boobs?"

"I haven't felt them!" she laughed. "She's built like me."

"Okay, I guess I'd do her too."

A few days later, I called her friend. Ann told her I might call, and she had evidently told Linda all about me. We talked for a while, and things seemed to click. She invited me to a party the upcoming Saturday. She lived about two and a half hours away, but I said I'd go with her. She told me Ann had other plans with her husband and wouldn't be there.

I drove to her house. She had some snacks out and had opened a good bottle of red wine. Ann told her that's what I like. We talked an hour or so before we left for the party.

We got to an upscale house on the water and met the hosts. They were very welcoming and outgoing. It was a great party. Linda was introducing me to a lot of people. I kind of felt like she was showing me off a little. She was also getting more affectionate as she drank.

It was getting late. Linda suggested we head back to her house. It was late and we had been drinking, so she told me I ought to stay. And I did.

Linda was nice, but the drive was too far for anything to really work out long term. If she lived closer, something might have developed. Chemistry and timing were there, but convenience now entered the equation, and it wasn't going to work for me.

Finding someone to spend the rest of my life with is much more difficult than I ever expected. I think I got into the wrong line in the search for my last first date. It definitely wasn't the express lane. I wish there was a fast pass like at Disney World.

When I was younger, it was simpler. In high school, there were no kids to deal with, little baggage, and we were thinking idealistically about our goals and dreams. In college, dreams and goals become clearer and careers start to complicate things. Later, there are kids, exes, exes' families, differing goals and dreams, careers, logistics, and more baggage. There's a lot that has to go right for a middle-aged relationship to work. It's more than just timing and chemistry.

Next.

SQUEAKY

Courtney was a really easy to talk with. She spoke well, ran her own business, and had traveled extensively.

We made plans to meet for dinner, and I was running late. I had to drop my daughter off at her friend's house, and I underestimated how far out they lived and how long it would take. I texted Courtney to let her know.

I finally arrived twenty minutes late. I felt really bad and was kind of flustered about rushing and being tardy—that's not me. Usually I'm five minutes early. Courtney was very understanding and helped make me feel better about it.

She was very pretty—about five feet five, slender, with nice curves and long blonde hair with bangs. I thought she had a confident, classy demeanor and dressed well—kind of sexy but understated. Courtney was very calm and relaxed. And she smelled good too. The more we talked, the more we found we had a lot in common. We knew a lot of the same people, and she knew a lot of influential people in town.

We had a great time. She never had kids and asked a lot of questions about mine. We talked about each of our businesses. I was thinking there were ways we could help each other with referrals and introductions.

I kissed her good night at her car. When I kissed her, she made her lips squeak as the kiss was ending.

A week or so, we went out again, and I picked her up. Dinner and conversation was just as good as our first date. We were pretty comfortable with each other. As I took her home, she invited me in for a glass of wine.

We ended up making out on her couch. Every time we kissed, she squeaked out a kissing sound. The first or second time, it was kind of cute; but after that, it was kind of annoying. And her breath wasn't the freshest.

Then her little dog jumped on the couch, trying to get some attention. It was sitting on the top of the couch, licking my head. Okay, I can tolerate some bad breath for a while—and the sound effects—but not the dog. Time for me to go home.

I went out with her again and eventually ended up on her couch with the same scenario—squeaky lips, but no bad breath this time. I kind of chuckled to myself. I guess I could have said something about the sound effects, but I worked through it. I had taken my tie off earlier and had to look for it when I left. The dog had dragged it off and made a new, very expensive silk chew toy out of it.

Courtney and I got along great. We had common interests and similar personalities; it was pretty good. She seemed like someone I could have had a relationship with. We had several long conversations, and we spent some quality time together. She was good for me in many ways, and she was very nice, but there just wasn't the spark I was looking for. I tried, but I just didn't get the feeling. I almost felt like I was about to try to force it, and I knew that wouldn't work.

Maybe I couldn't get past the squeaky lips.

"Jenny, another dog ate my clothes . . ."

"You're the only person I know who could say that," she laughed.

Sad but true.

Next.

PLUS OR MINUS?

Lindsey looked cute in her pictures, and when I talked to her, she seemed perky and light-hearted. She was about forty and had been married once before, but she had no kids. She worked for a software company, and she seemed pretty smart.

The first time we went out, we had a really nice time. Lindsey had a great sense of humor. She really didn't take much too seriously. She was always smiling. The conversation flowed. We really didn't have much in common, but we found a lot of things to talk about. We laughed a lot, and we made plans to see each other again.

We talked and texted a few times over the next couple weeks until our next date. Lindsey seemed very sweet and caring. It was fun talking with her and getting to know her. She said she wasn't feeling well in the days leading up to our date, so I expected her to cancel.

I was waiting in the restaurant bar for Lindsey and saw her walk in. She smiled as she came over to me, but it wasn't the big smile she had before.

"How are you feeling?" I asked her.

"I'm okay," she said.

"I'm getting a glass of wine. What would you like?"

"I'd like a Coke please. I need to use the restroom."

"How was your day?" she asked when she got back.

"It was pretty good. I opened a new account and did a little business. I like those kinds of days."

"Good for you."

"You still seem under the weather," I told her. She definitely wasn't the same bubbly woman as she was last time.

"Yeah, I am."

"Have a cold or touch of flu?"

She looked at me with tears welling in her eyes and said, "I'm pregnant."

What? Danger! Danger! That's why she wasn't feeling well. Lindsey was obviously having a hard time about it.

"What happened?" I asked. Well, I wasn't there, but I knew what happened. What a stupid question to ask.

"I was with my old boyfriend about a month ago. The day after, we ended it for good. And now I'm pregnant. I was told I couldn't have kids. Oh, God!" And with that, the tears were flowing

I gave her my handkerchief.

"What are you going to do?"

"I don't know. I always wanted a child."

"That's a lot of responsibility."

"I know."

Wow. I really didn't know what to say to her. It's not exactly a situation I ever thought I'd be in.

"Have you ever thought about having a family?" she asked.

"I have a family—a son and two daughters."

"No, I mean another family."

"Not really. Why?"

"You're a really great guy. Would you date a pregnant woman? And keep seeing me after I have a baby?"

Okay, now what? All I can do is be honest. And being honest isn't always easy, but it's always the right thing to do.

"Lindsey, you're a nice woman. But I've had kids, and they're almost grown and on their own. I'm at a different stage in my life, and I really don't want to be a daddy again. I had a vasectomy. I don't date women with young children or who want to have kids. I'm honest about it. I like my freedom. That's just where I am. I'm sorry."

She looked at me with more tears rolling down her face.

"I know you'd still be a good dad," she said. "Most guys wouldn't be that honest. They'd lie and then run."

I learned later that Lindsey moved in with a man a few months before she gave birth. I hope she found someone who would take care of her and her child.

Talk about baggage. I wasn't being selfish. I barely knew this girl. It's not that I didn't have compassion for her; it's just not a situation I wanted to get into.

"How was your date last night?" Jenny asked.

"She's pregnant," I replied.

"Oh my god! What?"

"Long story. But it's not mine."

Next.

ROACH!

Sally called me at around 4:00 p.m. She invited me to meet her and some of her friends after work that day for drinks and sushi at a place not far from my office downtown. It was short notice, but I didn't have any plans, so I went.

When I got there, Sally and her friends were already sitting at a table. There were seven of them, three guys including me. Sally got up and welcomed me with a hug. I think she stood on tiptoes to hug me. She might be five feet three in five-inch platform heels, and I'm about six feet two. And she might have been all of 110 lbs.

Besides being short, she was cute, with a dark complexion, brown eyes, and a lot of long straight black hair. And she was so top-heavy, I don't know how she could keep her balance in the wind on those high heels. Whenever I saw her, she was always dressed professionally, though.

Her friends were fun. Everyone was having a good time. I was probably ten to fifteen years older than them, but no one seemed to notice but me.

It's funny how a few drinks can affect people. After several beers, one of the guys who was in a white starched shirt and tie thought he really needed to show off his sleeve of ink and a tattoo on his chest.

Two of the girls decided to tell us about some guys they met in a club the previous weekend and about recent hook-ups. The guy I thought might be gay decided to come out of the closet.

I had little to add to the scene. Okay, maybe I was too old for this crowd. I think I'll eat more sushi. I needed to see if I could get more low-sodium soy sauce.

Sally was talking with them all too. It was funny to watch the interaction with the topics of conversation. The gay guy knew a lot about shoes. Everyone was getting more and more "loose".

By now, Mr. Tattoo was flirting heavily with one of the club girls at the end of the table, and she was flirting back. The other club girl seemed slightly miffed she wasn't being hit on, but she found her way to talk with the rest of us.

Sally was trying to keep up with the drinking of the rest of people at the table. At her size, I couldn't believe her alcohol tolerance was very high. And it was starting to show.

Okay, one more piece of sushi. I was having fun; this was entertaining.

By now, tattoo boy and club girl were making out at the end of table. No one seemed to pay any attention to them. The other club girl mentioned something about texting a guy for a bootie call later that night.

It was a weeknight, and everyone had to work the next day, so we wrapped up and started to leave. The make-out couple took off like a shot and were gone before we all stood up.

As the rest of us were walking outside, Sally started screaming—loudly.

"Aaahhh! Get it off me!" And she started freaking out.

"What?" we all asked.

Sally was doing a dance, and her arms were flailing all over the place.

"Roach! Get it!" Her dance continued, and her shirt was coming off.

It was well-lit outside, and we didn't see any roach.

She was well into a full-blown meltdown.

"Aaahhh! F*cking!"

She was quite a sight, trying to brush off a roach that had evidently crawled into her shirt—arms going, mouth going, balancing on her heels, and breasts giggling. It was hard not to laugh. Others gathered around to see what the commotion was all about.

She finally calmed down.

No one saw a bug crawl off. One of her friends was shaking out her shirt, and there was nothing. We looked all over her and the sidewalk, but there was no bug.

"I still feel it—right here," she said as she pointed to the back of her shoulder. "Get it! Get it! I *hate* roaches!"

There was no roach. Some of her hair was stuck in her bra strap, which seemed to be tickling her shoulder.

Now we were all laughing—even her.

There she was, standing on busy Main Street in a skirt, a bra, at least four-inch heels, more than a bit flustered, a bit tipsy, and trying not to show her embarrassment.

I told them all good night.

I saw that Mandy and some of her friends had been watching. They were laughing too, and Jenny heard all about it the next day.

After you see a bug, don't you sometimes seem to feel something crawling on you? I did—all the way home. Then I started laughing again.

Next.

AMAZON ENGINEER

Lydia contacted me through Match, and we talked a few times. She was some kind of an engineer with a big company. She really didn't like talking about her work; she said it was boring, and she was right. I think what she did may have been classified defense work.

When we talked, she seemed a bit eclectic but nice. She sent me photos of herself with color treatments and abstract effects. Lydia seemed like she was an analytical engineer by day and someone with a very artsy side by night.

We met after work one day, and I was more than a bit surprised. Her profile said she was six feet tall with an athletic and toned body. When I saw her, she was about six feet five with her heels, and her shoulders were as wide as a linebacker. Lydia was easily two hundred pounds and bigger than most men. She towered over me. Maybe she was previously a man.

Her dress tried to flatter her curvy figure. There was a lot of woman there. She wasn't exactly what I was expecting, nor was she really my type. I was already disengaged.

The conversation was all over the place; she was very quirky. It was obvious she was intelligent, but at the same time she was immature. She went from talking about her work as an engineer to her art interests, to being a seductress and talking about her lover then to her pets—while her voice sometimes changed to that of a little girl. It seemed like she had ADD too.

What? She said she has a lover?

"Why are you out dating when you already have a lover?" I asked her.

"He only satisfies me sexually. It's not a relationship," she said. "He's a former football player. I want a relationship, and a little voice tells me I won't get that from him. I know that. I have a woman I see once in a while too."

I think Lydia should explore the possibility of a relationship with the voices in her head. Why did she need two lovers? Don't most women just get a toy? This just keeps getting more bizarre. Jerry Springer must be close again.

There seemed to be a serious internal conflict and insecurity going on with this woman. She kept telling me to kiss her. I didn't. At first I thought she was a bit different. Now I thought she was wacked out.

I was wondering what kind of medication she was on, and if the home knew she was out.

It was kind of creepy. There had to be hidden cameras watching. Combine that with her physical looks—and I was not interested.

Check, please.

As we said goodbye outside the restaurant, she asked me to go to a party with her the next weekend. I declined. Then she asked me to grab her crotch and kiss her. I said goodbye and walked away. The Rick James song "Super Freak" popped into my head.

I told Jenny about Lydia.

"Where did you meet this one?" she asked.

"Online."

She just laughed.

"You might want to look over your shoulder. Sounds like this one could be a psycho stalker," she said. "And you need to stop going online."

She was probably right. But I'm a guy—we don't always listen very well.

Next.

STORY TIME

Kristin and I messaged back and forth a few times. I think I only talked to her once before we actually met, and it was a fairly brief conversation. I went into our date not knowing much about her, and not much rapport was built. I really didn't like that.

We met for drinks after work north of town, closer to where she worked. I didn't know the wine bar she recommended, but it was nice.

When she came in, I could tell the pictures she had posted were taken at least a few years ago. She looked older than her pictures—with a few more wrinkles and a bit more of a weathered look. I know women wouldn't want to be referred to as weathered, but she looked it. She was still attractive, just not exactly what I was expecting.

We sat down and ordered a glass of wine.

"So what's your story?" she asked.

"My story?"

"Yeah, what are you looking for?"

"Wow. That's pretty deep stuff to start with for a shallow guy like me," I said with a laugh.

I tried to get her involved in a conversation about her work, family, and travels. I wanted her to talk so I could learn more about her. I didn't care what she did or where she had traveled; I wanted to learn about her and hear how she talked. Could she hold a conversation? What kind of experiences had she had? How does she express herself?

But she seemed more focused on learning about me. It was like she had a mental list of questions to which she wanted answers. Or maybe she was more to the point as a result of being hardened by years of dating. Either way, I didn't particularly like it.

"What makes you different?" she asked.

"I don't know. Different from what?"

"You know, what makes you tick?"

"I really don't know. I think that's for a woman to decide as she gets to know me."

"What are you looking for in a woman? Or are you just into the sex?" she asked.

"I don't know exactly what I'm looking for, but I'll know it when I find it."

"Boy, that's a cop-out if I've ever heard one!" she said. "You're like all the rest. That means you're just playing the field."

"How can you say that? You don't even know me," I replied.

"I've heard that line before. See, you're all the same."

"You're kind of judgmental, aren't you?"

"No, just experienced."

"Do you know exactly what you're looking for? Finding someone isn't like ordering on a Chinese menu where you order something from column one and something from column two then you get two sides and a cookie," I told her.

"I know."

"How many men have you really gotten to know?"

"I can usually tell everything I need to know about a guy from the first date."

"So how many?"

"I don't know. A few."

"What happened?"

"After a couple of dates, they all turn out to be pigs."

"You don't seem like you really give anyone a break. How many men have you dated in the last year?"

"Fifteen or so."

"And not one was worth dating more than a couple of times?"

"Nope."

"Think it might be your approach?"

I guess I had three heads again. I got that look from her.

"You don't come across as friendly. You know the old saying? You attract more flies with honey than vinegar. There has been no honey and a lot of vinegar since I met you tonight."

"I'm nice!"

"I'm sure you are, but it doesn't come across. You come across as a hard-ass, and you seem judgmental and jump to conclusions quickly."

"I've been doing this a while, and following my gut works for me."

"It works so well, you haven't dated anyone more than a couple of times in over a year. How long have you been online dating?"

"A couple of years."

"And nothing? Yeah, I can see how well it's working for you."

"You don't need to be mean."

"I'm sorry. I'm not trying to be. You already reached a conclusion about me. I was just asking questions to learn about you. And I'm not trying to be mean, but how old are the pictures on your Match profile?"

"About five years."

"You don't look exactly like your pictures. You should update them so guys know what to expect."

"Are you calling me old?"

"No, I'm saying you need to be more honest. If a guy comes to meet you, and you don't look like your picture, they may be surprised or disappointed. Then you come at them like a hard ass, and you'll never get to know anyone."

"What are you talking about?"

"If you don't look like your picture, the guy gets pissed. Then you drill him first thing with questions about what he is looking for. Most guys will get defensive, and you'll never get to know them. Your cynicism comes shining through and it acts like a good-guy repellant."

"So you're saying it's me? You're being mean."

"No, it's just something you may want to think about. You're not giving anyone a chance to know you and like you."

"I guess you're being what you think is honest, even if it is mean. I suppose that makes you different," she said.

"I think I'm different, but don't we all? And you'll never get to really know what kind of a guy I am. I bet some of the other guys you dated were pretty good guys too, but you never gave them a chance either. And you turned them off. Are you afraid of relationships, or getting to know a guy, or a guy getting to know you?"

"Now who's being deep?"

And from there, we pretty much wrapped it up. Amazing what can happen in a thirty-minute date. I was exhausted and ready to go home.

I never heard from Kristin again. I hope she finds what she was looking for. Who knows, maybe something I said to her will help her find her happiness. And she needed some happiness.

Sometimes we get what we deserve. Some get lucky and get better than they deserve—that's what I'm hoping for.

Next!

TEACHER

"Who are you meeting for lunch today?" Jenny asked as I was about to leave the office.

"Lauren. She's a teacher."

So off I went to meet Lauren.

We had talked a couple of times. She had a couple of kids and they had just returned from a vacation at the beach. She seemed nice.

Lauren and I met at a restaurant not far from my office. We said our hellos, and when she smiled, I couldn't help but notice how bad her teeth were. I think she had all of her teeth; they were just crooked, twisted, and discolored. I don't remember seeing her teeth in her profile pictures. I'd probably keep my mouth closed for pictures too.

We were seated and talking, but I had already checked out. I tried to be conversant and pleasant, but it didn't matter. I tried not to look at her mouth, but it was hard. How did she brush and floss those things? I thought about referring her to my kids' orthodontist. I felt sorry for her that she had to go through life like that—it probably wasn't her fault.

I had to get back to my office for a meeting.

I don't know if she was not in the financial position to get her teeth corrected or not. She was a nice person, but I couldn't get past the teeth. I didn't mean to be shallow, but I guess I was in this regard.

When I got back to the office, I saw Mandy.

"Has anyone told you that you really have a great smile?" I asked her, and she beamed those straight pearly whites of hers.

I needed that.

Next.

TEST

Whenever my sixteen—and thirteen-year-old daughters needed money, I'd have them come over and clean my house. I hated to just give it to them. I wanted them to earn it and learn the value of work and money. While cleaning one day, my older daughter found a pair of Brad Paisley concert tickets on my kitchen counter.

She texted me: "Which one of us are you taking to see Brad Paisley?"

Me: "Neither."

Her: :(

Both of my daughters were Brad Paisley and country music fans. So was Danielle.

I bought the tickets for Danielle and me to go, and I told Danielle the story.

"We should take your girls," Danielle told me.

"Really? Okay. I'll get them some cheap seats," I said.

"Then we use the cheap seats and they get the good ones."

Hmm. Not exactly what I had in mind. Guess I was getting the girls some good seats—and I did. Thank you Stub Hub.

A few weeks later, we all rode together to the concert for the hour-long ride.

The girls' seats were better than ours. They were way up front—a couple of seats off the stage that jetted out into the audience. The girls were so excited after they got seated. During the first band, whoever had the two seats between them and the stage wasn't there yet, so they scooted over to be stage front.

Danielle and I sat a couple of sections away, but we could see them. I wanted to keep my eye on them as a protective dad.

When the second band finished, my cell phone rang. It was my older daughter.

"Daddy, can I talk to Danielle?"

I handed my phone to her. They talked for less than a minute.

"They want me to meet them by the food court," Danielle said.

I tried to give her some money in case they wanted food, but she wouldn't take it. I didn't think too much of them wanting Danielle to meet them.

A few minutes later, she was back.

"I thought they wanted a tampon or something. They wanted me to buy them a margarita!" she said.

"Did you?"

"Yes. I hope you don't mind."

"Not really," I said.

I did kind of mind though. I give them sips of my drinks occasionally, but I never gave them a whole drink, let alone bought them one in public. One daughter was sixteen and the other thirteen.

Brad Paisley came out and gave a great show. Afterward, we found the girls, and they were holding their souvenir drink cups. The cups looked like they would hold about a quart. My girls were silly. I wasn't mad—it was kind of funny.

We stopped at a convenience store for drinks on the ride back. Inside, my girls asked if they could get a snack. The younger one wanted ice cream. The older one brought to the counter a Dr. Pepper and a big bag of Doritos, and the younger one had lemonade and a pint of Ben & Jerry's ice cream. They had the munchies.

The next day, I called my older daughter to check on them, subtly asking if they had a hangover.

"Daddy, I don't like Danielle," she said.

"Why?"

"We gave her a test last night, and she failed."

"What do you mean?"

"We asked her to buy us drinks as a test, and she did—and she failed!"

"Now wait a second," I said. "She came back and told me she bought you drinks. I failed. I should have come over and took them from you, but I didn't want to embarrass either of you girls or Danielle."

"You put Danielle in a lose-lose situation," I continued. "If she buys you a drink, she does wrong and loses. If she doesn't, you think she's a bitch and she loses. Do you see that? She was trying to be cool for you two. You shouldn't do that. It's not fair. You were wrong."

"Yeah, I guess," she said.

Come Monday in the office, I said, "Hey, Jenny. What would you think if one of my dates bought my girls some margaritas?"

"What?"

Not quite next.

DANIELLE—PART 2

A few days after that, Danielle came over to my house with her son to ride Jet Skis on the lake. It was a beautiful day. The sun was shining and there was a slight breeze—a good day to be on the lake.

I was still getting the Jet Skis ready to ride and gassed up when they arrived. Danielle and her son, John, looked ready for fun.

I took them down to the dock, and John was immediately on a Jet Ski. But I had the keys in my pocket. John was about thirteen.

"Let's go!" John yelled. "Come on!"

"I have to teach you how to drive it and how to be safe—and my rules," I told him.

"I know how," he said. He was a know-it-all teenager.

"You have to listen to him, John," his mom told him.

"Have you ever been on a Jet Ski?" I asked him.

"I rode on the back of one with my dad about three years ago."

"Okay, then you don't know much. Until you pay rent, you have to pay attention," I told him.

So I went over on how to operate it. John wanted the fast one, but I let Danielle use that one and John got the slower one. And the slower one could still get up to fifty-five miles per hour! But I was using the training key on it, which would only let it go about thirty miles per hour.

"When you come in, you have to be coasting when you reach the dock and let it idle to the beach, okay? Remember, these things don't have brakes." I told John.

"Okay. I got this."

I pushed Danielle from the beach, and she took off. I pushed John, and off he went, but he turned and looked at me. He turned it around and came back to the beach.

"It's not working," he complained.

"Yes, it is."

"No, it's not. It's not going like Mom's."

"That's because I have it set to go slower—to be safe."

"That's not fair! I can handle it! Make mine go fast!"

"Show me you can be safe first."

"This sucks!" And he got off and went on the dock pouting.

Danielle came back to see what was wrong. She told John they were my Jet Skis—so my rules. And she reminded him that I told him I would let him go faster if he proved to me that he could be safe.

He griped and complained like a thirteen-year-old boy does. And after he realized he wasn't going to win, he finally got back on and rode with the slow key.

We watched him from the dock. Every time he came by, he asked if he could go faster yet. Danielle went out and rode by him. I think her going faster than him just made him mad, but he was riding safely.

They both came in, and John was begging to go faster. I asked Danielle if it was okay with her, and it was.

"John, this thing goes fast, and it can be very dangerous. You can hurt yourself badly if you go too fast and don't pay attention," I said. I forgot I was talking to a thirteen-year-old. I don't think he heard a word I said. Anyway, off he went.

We watched him from the dock, and I waved him in.

"What?" he asked as he rode up.

"You're going too fast! You don't have enough experience to ride that fast. If you don't slow down, I'll put the kiddie key back on it."

"It's not too fast!"

"He'll be fine," Danielle said.

Okay. If he breaks his neck, it will be his fault, but I'm still the one getting sued. Off he went.

He was kind of going slower—but not much. He kept looking at us to see if we were watching him. He was smiling and having a good time.

Danielle and I went inside to get drinks and cool off. A few minutes later, John walked in.

He looked at me and asked, "Can I talk to you for a second?"

Uh-oh.

"Okay." And I went outside with him.

He didn't need to say a word. I saw that my Jet Ski was in the middle of my backyard.

My neighbor, Mark, was walking to the Jet Ski. We walked out there too. Danielle had just come outside.

"Oh my god!" she said. "What did you do, John?"

"He was going about forty-five miles per hour when he hit the beach and went airborne," Mark explained.

Mark was sitting on his dock and said he watched the whole thing. And now my Jet Ski was about fifty feet from shore.

John knew he was in trouble. I was upset but not yelling-mad.

"I trusted you. Now I don't," I told John.

"But it wasn't my fault!" he said.

"Who was driving it?"

"Me."

"So why is it not your fault? Whose fault is it then?"

"I made a mistake!"

"Yes, you did. You didn't respect my rules. And you could have really hurt yourself. If you had landed at an angle, you could have rolled it right over you."

I don't think he realized the seriousness of what had happened. He was fine, so he thought it was no big deal. It was all the four of us could do to push it back to the water.

Against my better judgment, I let Danielle talk me into letting John ride more—but with the kiddie key. John refused and pouted the rest of the day.

I didn't see much of Danielle after that. My girls and her, her son and me—it wasn't going to work out. And I never told her about the $1,400 needed to fix the cracked hull on the Jet Ski that John caused.

Next.

Taxi!

Dina was recently divorced. She had been a stay-at-home mom most of her married life and was just getting back into the working mom routine. After talking a few times, we agreed to meet for lunch on a Saturday.

About an hour before I was supposed to meet Dina, she called saying she was having car troubles. She told me she had someone coming to look at her car later that day and asked if I could pick her up for lunch. I didn't live far away, so I agreed.

I got to her house a few minutes before 12:00 noon, and she was ready to go. And so was her son.

"You wouldn't mind if we drop Derek off at soccer practice, would you?" she asked. "It's not so far out of the way."

Derek was standing there in his practice gear, with an equipment bag, staring at me.

"No problem." What was I supposed to say?

We dropped him off and headed to lunch.

We went to lunch not too far away because she let me know we had to pick Derek back up after practice at 2:00 p.m., and we couldn't be late because the coaches get mad when parents were late. Okay, got it. Can't be late.

Dina was having a hard time getting into the flow of her new role as working mom. She went from being a homemaker to a single working mom. When I got to her house, there was laundry all over the couch and dishes piled high in the sink.

I found while talking with her at lunch that she was overwhelmed with the responsibilities of work and being a mom. She thought she had to do everything like she did as a homemaker, like gourmet dinners, dance and music lessons for her two kids, volunteering, and now add to that a full time job—and it was getting the best of her. She had to learn to prioritize, but that wasn't for me to tell her. She had to figure that out on her own.

She kept looking at her watch to make sure we finished lunch and had time to get Derek from soccer practice—and we did.

"Can we stop at the 7-Eleven up here? I need to pick up a gallon of milk," she said.

"Sure."

As she was getting out of the car, she said, "I forgot my purse. Can I borrow $5?"

All I had was a couple of $20 bills, so I handed her one.

She and her son came out with the milk. She had a Coke and some peanut M&M's, and he had a Gatorade and a bag of chips. She told me she also bought a Lotto ticket for that night's drawing. I never got any change back, nor did I expect to get a share if she won Lotto.

As we got back to her neighborhood with Derek in tow, Dina waived to her daughter who was walking to her house with some friends. Dina said she was coming home from one of the other girl's house for a birthday party. Our date was planned around her kids' schedules.

"Hey, my ex-husband doesn't live far from you, would you mind dropping them off at his house on your way home?" she asked. This time, both of her kids were standing there, staring at me.

That was kind of presumptuous, but her car was not working, and I'm a nice guy. Besides, they were staring at me.

"No problem."

The ride to their dad's was pretty awkward. Here was a nine-year-old and a twelve-year-old who I just met, trusted to me from a woman I just met, taking them to a man I didn't know. The kids didn't talk much. Luckily, it was less than a fifteen-minute drive.

As I drove into their dad's driveway, I saw him working in the front yard, waiting for them. He looked up at us—it was Ken. He was an acquaintance from an organization we both belonged to. It just got a whole lot more awkward.

"Hi, Ken," I said.

"Hey. Dina said her date was giving the kids a ride over here. I wasn't comfortable with that, but she said you had already left. I'm glad it was you instead of some stranger. Thanks for bringing them over."

"No problem. I didn't know she was your ex-wife. I wouldn't have seen her if I knew."

"Don't worry about it. I'd say go for it, but I wouldn't do that to someone I liked. You know, never sell a used car to someone you know? The only thing I'll say is run, run away, and run far."

"Okay," I said as we both laughed.

It was still pretty awkward. Especially with the kids standing there, staring at us.

Next!

SISTERS

I was online and saw a picture of someone who looked familiar. I reached out to her, and it turned out that we had met each other before. We had met at a business function a year or so earlier. Alexa and I soon made plans to meet after work.

She was in the public relations/advertising business. She was pretty and about ten years younger than me, but she seemed much more mature. She had a lot of business contacts that could help my business. And Alexa was a good conversationalist—she was interesting and smart.

We were just getting our second glass of wine when we heard a woman yell, "What a waste!"

We both looked up. Alexa smiled.

"What happened?" Alexa said to the woman.

"What a total waste of time," she said. "He was a total loser!"

Alex introduced me to her younger sister, Crystal.

"What happened?" I asked.

"I was on a blind date. I met this guy down the street—and he was boring, had bad breath, didn't know how to dress, and had on a God-awful cologne. I thought my nose was going to catch fire. He was just a slob."

"That describes most of them," Alexa said. "What was his name?"

Most of them? Hello! I'm right here!

"Chris something. He works in finance or banking or something like that," Crystal said.

"Chris Johnson?" I asked.

"Yeah, that's him, I think. Do you know him?"

"Kind of," I replied. It was the Chris I work with. I just smiled and chuckled inside.

And with that, Alexa and Crystal were chatting like, well, sisters.

"He wasn't as bad as your date a couple of weeks ago, though," Crystal said.

"Oh, you got that right!" Alexa laughed. "Talking about losers, what about that cop you went out with?"

"Thanks for reminding me!"

I love this walk down the memory lane they were taking me on—not.

A few minutes later, it turned.

"You must not be too bad if Alexa is still here with you," Crystal said to me.

"Thanks."

"So how did you two meet?" Crystal asked. "What do you do? Where are you from?" And on and on it went.

All the questions I just answered to Alexa, I now was going over with Crystal. I felt like I was on a first date with two girls.

Hmmm. I was kind of dating sisters at the same time? Many possibilities were going through my mind. I wonder if they felt like a sandwich. Okay, okay, back to reality.

Ever since Crystal showed up, the date went downhill. It was no longer about me and Alexa. It was now about two sisters talking and giggling. I was now the third wheel. It was entertaining listening to them, though.

They talked about Crystal's failed date—how she always found losers, how she was jealous because Alexa got the good guys. And I heard about several of them. Oh, joy.

Alexa left for the ladies' room, and Crystal says, "Have you ever been with sisters before?" She definitely had a sparkle in her eye and a devilish grin.

"No."

"Ever thought about it? Like me and Alexa?"

"Of course I've thought about it! I'm a guy. If you were twins, it would be even more interesting. But I wouldn't."

"Why not?" she said, and she became very flirtatious.

"Is that something you and Alexa have done before?" I asked.

"No, not with Alexa. She's my sister! I was just seeing what you'd say."

"I'm glad I didn't fall into your trap."

Crystal just smiled.

As Alexa came back to our table, she said, "Were you trying to steal my date again?"

"Don't go there," Crystal replied.

"What? You steal your sister's dates?" I asked.

"No! I met one, and he just liked me more than her."

"She stole him. And he was nice. Too nice for her, and he left her after their second date. She thinks taking my date is like borrowing my sweater," Alexa stated.

No sibling rivalry here.

"So neither of you got him. Why didn't you two tag team him?" I asked. "Then you could have both had him."

Crystal smiled again at me. "How about it, sis?"

"I don't share well. Besides, Crystal wouldn't know what to do with a good guy. She never listens. Party girl here wants a nice guy but always ends up with loser party boys. And usually she's juggling two or three at a time."

"I think I'm a good guy."

"You are. And that's why you're with me, not her."

Crystal just rolled her eyes.

"He's kind of cute," Crystal said as she nodded toward me.

"Yeah, but I'd change his hair," Alexa replied.

Hello! I'm right here! And I like my hair.

"He has nice shoes, though," said Crystal.

"He's nice, but I don't get all of his humor," Alexa replied.

Hello! I'm still here! I'm not sure I wanted to hear what they would say about me when I wasn't there.

They were having fun, and I just watched.

As we finished our second glass of wine, I called it a night.

The next day in the office, I asked Chris, "How was your date last night?"

"She wasn't my type," he responded.

I told him I was out with the sister of his date, and she met up with us after his date with Crystal ended.

"She said you might want to go lighter on the cologne and heavier on the mouthwash."

"Hmm," he grunted.

I talked with Alexa a couple of times after that night, but we never went out again. She was nice and had a lot to offer, but there really wasn't a spark for a relationship. We are very friendly when we see each other occasionally at different business functions though. She'll be a great catch for someone, just not for me. Her sister, well, she'll find someone too—just not sure exactly what.

Next.

BIG GAME

It was 6:30 on a Saturday evening, my favorite college football team was playing in an hour, and my TV cable was out. The cable company said they were working on it, but it would be several hours before they thought it would be repaired.

It was a big game. And I was hungry. Time to scramble.

I drove by a couple of sports bars, and they were packed. I didn't feel like being in a big crowd. I kept driving and remembered a nicer restaurant that had a bar area and a couple of TVs. And they had great food.

I walked into the restaurant, and it was perfect—it was a quiet restaurant without many kids, and the bar area wasn't full. I found a barstool that had a good view of the TV. I got there ten minutes before kick-off.

I ordered some food, got a drink, and was glad the barstool was comfortable since I was going to be in it for the next three and a half hours.

The game was close and exciting, and I was into it. The bar got busier with some others who came in to watch the game. A group of women also came in for drinks and sat in the empty stools next to me.

They were having a good time, and I was pretty much focused on the game. But I found one of the women quite beautiful. I just kept watching the game.

The women were talking and changing seats, and the pretty one was now sitting by me. She was talking to her friends. It was total girl talk—about their kids, their jobs, and gossip about their friends who weren't there. Someone they were talking about was evidently barefoot because she didn't have any shoes nor did she have a real purse.

"Go!" I said as a big play was happening.

"Who's playing?" she asked me.

"Florida State and Miami," I told her.

"My daughter went to FSU for a while."

"Cool. I went there too."

We smiled, and she went back to her friends.

A few minutes later, she turned back to me, and we chatted. She was in the medical field, had a couple of daughters, and was glad to be out of the house and out with her friends. She was pretty, about five feet three, slim, with beautiful green eyes—it was like they glowed in the light. She was also about my age. She told me her name was Brooke.

She went back and forth from her friends and me. They soon decided to go somewhere else to meet some other friends. She gave me her number before they left.

I was back to the game. I was never so glad my cable had gone out before.

A couple of days later, I called Brooke. In fact, we talked several times and eventually went out.

She was divorced with a couple of grown kids, and a couple of younger kids she had adopted as babies. Her job was treating cancer patients. She had a big heart, and she obviously really cared about others.

We started seeing each other, and things were going good. There were highs and lows as with every relationship, but things were really good. I helped her through things, and she helped me too. She's there for me, and I'm there for her. She has a smile that melts me. She really liked doing things for others, including me, as long as it didn't get in the way of her shoe shopping.

It's been over a year now, and things are still great with Brooke. She respects me and supports my work and my relationship with my kids. And I think I'm good for her too. No wacked-out stories, no weirdness. In fact, there's nothing more I want to share about our private lives other than I think we are both happy. It's been a long time since I've been happy, and it feels good. Really good.

Is she perfect? No, but neither am I, but she likes me anyway. Together we are great.

I feel loved.

And I think I finally had my last first date.

No more "Next."

CONCLUSION

What can you say about my dates? I know some may question the events, but I'm not creative enough to make them up. I'm an analytical guy, not creative. People say fact is stranger than fiction—I know. I lived it. I still believe I was unknowingly being filmed for some sort of future reality show. I look back at some and still cannot believe them.

Why did I date so many women? Don't women say they have to kiss a lot of frogs to find a prince? Why would it be any different for guys?

I'm an optimist. I knew there was someone special for me out there. I wasn't going to settle, and I knew I wouldn't be happy if I did. I knew what I wanted, and I wasn't going to wait for it to fall out of the sky. I had to keep looking for the one. I had to keep trying. And I met many more women than I've written about here.

I hate dating. First dates seem like a job interview. It was exhausting. I couldn't wait for my last first date. I also found dating is expensive! I hope women appreciate and understand what a gentleman does (or is supposed to do) for a date. It's a shame that most women don't. Thankfully, some women do appreciate it. Seem like most women are looking for a good time instead of a good man.

And it's amazing how some women had great jobs, good educations, social stature, but many still lacked real class. Having a nice dress, great shoes, jewelry, and an expensive purse may make you look classy; but it does not make you classy. It's like manners and etiquette are things of the past. Some men and women are more into show and style over substance. I wanted substance.

While many of the stories are bizarre, funny, or boring, most of the women I met, I think, meant well. I met a lot of women who all had stories, lives, jobs, families, exes, and other issues—all of which creates baggage. The older we get, the more baggage we all have. It's life. Some use it to create drama, others adapt and more forward.

And not all of the women I met were kooks, crazies, and loose. I learned "normal" is a relative term. I met some very nice women who would make a great wife or a great mother, and some I became friends with. In the majority of cases, there just wasn't a spark or interest in taking anything further. Sometimes it was on my side, sometimes it was on hers, sometimes it was mutual. Over time, I became more comfortable with it, but I still hate dating.

As you've read, the dating world is treacherous, but it can also be fun. And it can be rewarding at any age. Online dating is not for the faint of heart. There is someone out there for everyone. Several of the women I met are now engaged to be married or are married, and I wish them a lifetime of happiness.

But you have to be out there to find someone and kiss a lot of frogs before you find your match.

Relationships are something that cannot be forced and not a decision that should be rushed into. Some women are looking for Superman before they are over their last Superman.

These experiences helped me realize how different we all are. We all think that we are normal and everyone else is weird. I saw more different types of people, personalities, and backgrounds than I ever thought were out there. It expanded my horizons, and I think it helped me become a little more sensitive to others—trying not to be judgmental despite their behavior at times. Just smile, laugh, try not say to anything, and roll with the punches. Life is what you make of it.

There are no perfect people or perfect relationships. Some people hold out for Mr. or Ms. Perfect, and think they will be settling for something less. If that's their attitude, I think they could miss out on something special. Settling doesn't mean settling for less than perfect—it means settling for something that doesn't make you happy. Isn't happiness what we're all looking for?

About the woman I wrote of in the introduction who was searching for Mr. Wonderful, I never met her. But in my experience, I realized that I may not be her Mr. Wonderful, but I believe there is a Mr. Wonderful out there for her. And I hope she finds him and the happiness we are all looking for.

If this was a movie, I'd like the last scene to be a wedding scene, where the preacher says you may kiss the bride, and I do. Then the picture fades out, and you see pictures of me and my bride having fun and growing old together while the credits roll.

I wish you luck in your search for your last first date and your happily ever after. Don't ever give up!

Made in the USA
Lexington, KY
11 March 2016